Christmas
Vows

Christmas Vows

Seasons of Faith, Book 4

Rebekah Lyn

Real Life Books & Media
Copyright © 2015 by Rebekah Lyn

Real Life Books & Media
329 Cheney Highway #230
Titusville, FL 32780
www.rebekahlynbooks.com

Publisher's Note: This is a work of fiction. Names, characters, places, and incidents are a product of the author's imagination. Locales and public names are sometimes used for atmospheric purposes. Any resemblance to actual people, living or dead, or to businesses, companies, events, institutions, or locales is completely coincidental.

Christmas Vows/Rebekah Lyn--1st ed.
Cover art by LLPix.
ISBN: 978-0692575628

Other Books by Rebekah Lyn

Seasons of Faith
Summer Storms
Winter's End
Spring Dawn
Christmas Vows

Coastal Chronicles
Julianne

Jessie Cole Trilogy
*Undaunted (*previously sold a*s Jessie)*
Destiny's Call

CHAPTER ONE

"That was a wonderful dinner, Lizzie." Emma pushed back from the table and carried her empty plate to the sink. Lizzie stood as well, dropping her linen napkin on the table and following her friend into the kitchen.

"You're braver than I am," said Stephanie, a petite young woman as she handed Lizzie her plate.

"Come on, Steph. I know you're a great cook." Lizzie bumped the woman with her shoulder.

"I've never even considered doing a whole turkey," Stephanie replied.

"You can't have Thanksgiving without turkey," Stephen said.

Stephanie shrugged. "I'm usually working, so I get whatever is available in the cafeteria."

Lizzie looked around the house, taking in the activities of her friends. Ian and Stephanie were working together to clear the table. In the living room, Jeffrey and Stephen had chosen a football game on the television and Ron was rearranging the furniture so everyone could have a place to sit.

"I'm glad we all have the day off," Lizzie said as she reached for a cloth to start drying dishes.

"Thanks for inviting me," Stephen called from the couch. "I haven't had a meal that good in ages."

"Don't let Chef Gustave hear you say that," Lizzie called back.

"It's a shame Mona had to work today." Stephanie set a bowl on the counter, swooping her finger through the dollop of remaining mashed potatoes. "Then you would have taken in all of the Concierge Club strays."

"You aren't strays," Lizzie protested.

Stephanie licked the mashed potatoes from her finger. "We're single and have no family here, I'd say that makes us strays."

Ian carried the turkey platter to the kitchen and slipped an arm around Lizzie as he told Stephanie, "You'll always be welcome in our home, stray or not."

Lizzie leaned into him and sighed. Hearing him talk about their home together made her heart beat a little faster.

"Have you decided where you're going to live after the wedding?" Stephanie said and passed another empty bowl to Emma.

Ian dropped a kiss on the top of Lizzie's head and moved back to the table. "I told Lizzie we can stay here as long as she wants. She's put a lot of work into this place and I don't want her to leave until she's ready."

"We've all put a lot of work into it," Lizzie corrected. "Without each of you this place would still be a wreck."

"If I'd known how much you were going to make me work, I might not have accepted your cookies," Jeffrey said without turning away from the football game.

Lizzie smiled at the memory of her first meeting with Jeffrey, delivering homemade cookies to his construction site. She had gone there hoping to get some tips on how to go about renovating the derelict house she'd found. It didn't seem possible that little more than a year had passed since then.

"Don't kid yourself," Ron chimed in. "I don't know anyone who's ever turned down Lizzie's baking."

"Speaking of baking, where's the pumpkin pie?" Ian asked.

"You can't be ready to eat dessert already," Stephanie exclaimed.

Ian rubbed his stomach. "I still have room for a sliver of pie."

Lizzie swatted at him with her dishtowel. "Let us finish cleaning up then I'll make some coffee and get the desserts out."

"All right." Ian sighed and joined Jeffrey and Stephen on the couch.

"Men, constant eating machines," Stephanie said.

"That's okay, I have a plan to make them work off all those calories."

Stephanie grinned. "Does your plan have anything to do with the sacks of rocks I noticed in the backyard?"

"Shh," Lizzie hissed with a conspiratorial wink.

"I think that's it," Emma announced ten minutes later, pulling the plug on the sink and rinsing the soap from her wrinkled brown hands.

Stephanie put away the last plate and closed the cabinet door. "I can't believe you haven't installed a dishwasher."

Lizzie leaned against the counter and brushed at the beads of sweat forming on her forehead. "I haven't had enough dinner parties to see the need for one, but after today I may have to consider it."

"Cleaning up is half the fun of entertaining," Emma said.

"We have different ideas of fun." Stephanie dropped down into a chair, fanning herself.

Emma chuckled. "Why don't I get the coffee started?"

"Thank you." Lizzie gave Emma a look she hoped conveyed the gratitude she felt. When she'd decided to host Thanksgiving at her house, she hadn't thought about how much work it would be. The hours of cooking on top of the long hours she'd been putting in at the hotel the past few weeks had her ready to drop at any second.

"Go sit down with the boys and I'll bring you a cup of coffee when it's ready." Emma made a shooing motion with her hands.

Lizzie squeezed into the remaining space on the sofa between Jeffrey and Ian. Ian wrapped his arm around her and she snuggled into his shoulder. "Who's winning?"

"Dallas is up by three," Ian said.

"It's only the second quarter, though," Stephen said. "Plenty of time for them to get the beating they deserve."

"Just because it's not Miami playing, doesn't mean you have to be so bitter." Jeffrey jabbed Stephen in the ribs.

"I didn't realize you were such a football fan, Stephen." Lizzie leaned forward so she could see him.

"I had stopped watching for a while, but now that I'm not working every Sunday, Jeffrey and I have been going to the Ale House to watch the games this season."

Lizzie leaned back and looked up at Ian. "Why don't you go out with them?"

"Because I'd rather spend the day with you. It's the only time we see each other these days."

She knew he hadn't meant to, but his words cut her. Tammy, the hotel's group manager, had left for Texas in April to care for her mother who'd fallen and broken her hip. The recovery process hadn't gone as well as expected and Tammy had resigned in June so she could make the move to Texas permanent.

A new group manager had been hired six weeks earlier, but he didn't seem to be catching on very quickly, and Lizzie was still doing the lion's share of the work, spending ten to twelve hours at the hotel, six days a week.

She felt a finger under her chin and then her head was tilted up so she looked into Ian's sapphire blue eyes. The world slowed down. The anxiety and the wall she'd been erecting at his words melted away.

"I didn't mean it that way. I know how hard you're working."

She nodded. He leaned down and brushed her lips.

"Hey, hey, enough of that," cried Stephanie. "Some of us are still digesting our meals."

Lizzie giggled and looked at her friend. "I guess that means you are skipping pie then."

"Pie? Is it time for pie?" Jeffrey jumped up and looked around.

Stephanie burst into laughter.

"What? It's been almost an hour since we finished eating."

The sound of whipped cream being sprayed from a can brought Stephen and Ian to their feet.

"Watch out, Emma; hungry men are about to stampede you," Stephanie warned.

Jeffrey led the charge to the kitchen counter where Emma had placed two pies, one pumpkin and one chocolate. Ron stepped aside with his plate already filled with a slice from each, a generous covering of whipped cream on both pieces.

Stephen looked over his shoulder at Lizzie. "I don't know if this is enough pie."

"I guess us girls will just have to make do with cake."

"Cake? There's cake, too? Where?" Jeffrey stopped, mid-slice.

"Hurry up, man." Ian reached for the pie server.

"I'm going to need a bigger plate," Jeffrey said.

Lizzie shook her head and stood up. "Finish what you have and then come back for the cake."

She opened the refrigerator and pulled a long pan from the bottom drawer removing its tin foil and setting it on the counter next to the pies.

"Coconut cake? You do know the way to a man's heart." Jeffrey grabbed a second plate and cut a large slice, then, a plate in each hand, made his way to the table.

"Eat up boys, you're going to need your energy."

Jeffrey lowered his fork. "Uh oh, what is this going to cost us?"

Ian looked from the cake to Lizzie. "This is about that project in the backyard, isn't it?"

"Well, I wouldn't want you guys to put on any weight before the wedding." Lizzie gave them an angelic smile.

"But football is on," Jeffrey protested. "Thanksgiving football."

"There will be plenty of time after the game for you to work," Lizzie assured him.

Stephen swallowed a bite of pie. "What exactly is this project?"

Lizzie smiled. "Nothing too big."

CHAPTER TWO

Twilight was fading into night as Ian put away the last shovel. Lizzie watched through the kitchen window as the men stomped their feet and brushed their hands on their pants, sprinkling the patio with dirt. Her gaze drifted to the completed project: a dry creek bed that served as a border for a flowerbed and ended at a pond where a small fountain bubbled.

Stephen led the way through the back door. "The next time Lizzie offers to make me dinner, I'm going to have to say no."

"At least you have that luxury," Ian said. "I have a feeling I'm going to be doing projects like this for the rest of my life."

"I'm getting too old for this." Ron accepted the glass of water she extended to him, and downed it in one long gulp.

"You're not old." Lizzie filled Ron's glass again. "Anyway, that was the last project on my list."

Jeffrey blew out a loud breath. "Thank goodness."

"She just asked you to spread a few rocks," Stephanie said.

"Sure, a few thousand rocks, in a specific pattern, but not too perfect so that it would still look natural. No problem." Jeffrey fell back on the couch.

"It looks wonderful, though," Lizzie said. "Thank you."

"Consider it my wedding gift to you," Jeffrey replied.

"Mine too," Stephen said.

"I'm hiring a landscaper for our next home." Ian set his cup in the sink and rubbed his shoulder.

Lizzie reached up to massage it. "Then I won't be able to look at the yard and think about all the people who mean so much to me. Now I look outside and I see the shrubs Ron first tamed from the jungle I found here. When I look at the patio I think of Mae and her son Avery who helped me level the area and place the pavers. Now the creek bed will always remind me of this Thanksgiving and each of you."

Her gaze moved from Ian to Jeffrey, then Stephen and Ron, then back to Ian.

"Well, when you put it that way I guess it doesn't seem like so much work." Ian leaned forward to kiss her.

"Speak for yourself," Jeffrey grumbled. "I'm pretty sure I've pulled a hamstring."

"I told you not to bend over like that," Stephen said.

"I think there's still some cake left," Stephanie cut in. "Would that make you feel better?"

Jeffrey lifted his head from the back of the sofa and looked at Stephanie. "It might; would you be a dear and bring me a piece?"

"Oh, brother." Stephanie shook her head, but moved toward the kitchen. "Can I get anything for the rest of you while I'm at it?"

"No, thanks," Stephen replied. "I think I'm going to head home and hit the hot tub."

"You have a hot tub?" Jeffery perked up.

"Not me personally," Stephen said, "but my apartment complex does."

"Oh." Jeffrey let his head drop back onto the couch cushion.

"I'll see you tomorrow," Lizzie said, giving Stephen a hug.

"I should get going too. I have the opening shift tomorrow," Stephanie said as she handed Jeffrey a plate with a large slice of cake, then she collected her purse from a table by the door.

"Thanks for coming, Steph." Lizzie embraced her friend, then stood at the door watching Stephen and Stephanie walk across the grass to their cars. She saw the pair stop in front of Stephanie's sporty little convertible, but couldn't hear what they were talking about. She felt the door move in her hand and turned to see Ian pressing it closed.

Ian pointed toward Lizzie's favorite chair. "Why don't we give them some privacy?"

Lizzie didn't budge. "What do you know that I don't?"

Ian shrugged. "It's more of a feeling than any real knowledge."

"We think Stephen has the hots for Stephanie," Jeffrey said around a mouthful of cake.

"Really?" Lizzie tried to think if she'd seen any signs of it herself.

"Like I said, it's only a feeling."

"It makes sense, though." Jeffrey set down his plate. "They have a lot in common and he has mentioned her a couple of times when we've been hanging out."

"But he only sees her at our Concierge Club dinners. That's once, maybe twice a month."

"Are you sure about that?" Jeffrey leaned forward, his elbows on his knees.

Lizzie moved to her chair, the leather molding to her body when she sat down. "I guess not. I didn't know the two of you were football buddies."

"Has Stephanie mentioned him?" Jeffrey asked.

"Not that I can think of, but we don't talk about our personal lives very much."

"Well, if she doesn't like him, then I hope she lets him down easy." Ian sat down on the couch and propped his feet on the edge of the coffee table. "He's a nice kid."

Emma chuckled. "He's only a few years younger than you."

"He's become kind of like a little brother to me," Jeffrey said.

Ron guzzled down another glass of water then joined Emma at the dining room table. "We've collected quite the family here, haven't we, my dear?"

Emma nodded. "Yes, we have."

Lizzie met Emma's gaze and felt a lump rise in her throat. These were the kind of moments when it was hardest to forget the painful loss of her parents in a terrible car accident. Emma and Ron, unable to have children of their own, had become surrogate parents to Lizzie over the past few years. She tried to smile at the woman who'd become a surrogate mother to her.

"We better head home, too. I have to be up early to get my Black Friday shopping done," and Emma stood and crossed the room to where Lizzie sat. "Thank you again for a lovely dinner."

The two women clasped hands and squeezed tightly. "Happy Thanksgiving," Lizzie whispered.

"See you Sunday." Ron settled a worn baseball cap on his bald head and opened the door.

"Love you guys." Lizzie waved as they walked out.

"That must be my cue to leave as well." Jeffrey reached for his sneakers.

"You don't have to go," Lizzie said.

"Why don't you call Michelle and see if she wants to come over to watch a movie?" Ian suggested.

Jeffrey pulled his shoes closer to the couch, but didn't move to put them on. "I don't think that's a good idea."

"Why not? I thought you two were getting along pretty well." Lizzie swung her legs over the side of the chair and scooted down so her head rested on the other arm.

"We get along fine," Jeffrey agreed. "If she hasn't opened up to the idea of a relationship with God by now, though, I don't know if she ever will, and I know I'm not strong enough to withstand temptation if I don't keep some distance between us."

"Well, yes, but look at how long it took *you* to become a believer," Ian said.

"I know, I know. I've spent a lot of time wondering how Camylle was so willing to tie her life to mine when we didn't share the same beliefs."

Ian nodded. "She was certain you'd come around eventually and thought, by loving you unconditionally, you'd better understand the love God has for us."

"Did she tell you that?"

"We talked about it a few times after the two of you got engaged. At first I worried she was making a mistake, but I could tell she was at peace about it and believed God had a plan."

Jeffrey's face clouded. "I wish it had been a different plan."

Ian touched Jeffrey's shoulder. "Me too, man. Me too."

"I understand if you just want to be friends with Michelle," Lizzie said, "but that doesn't mean you have to close yourself off from other relationships. There are a couple of women at our church we could introduce you to."

Jeffrey smiled. "You're just worried I won't have a plus one for the wedding and it'll throw off your seating."

"Ha, ha," Lizzie mocked. "Odd numbers are more difficult, but more than that I want you to be happy."

"I know you do." Jeffrey's smile faded. "I wish Michelle didn't have to be so stubborn. I do like her."

"Call and invite her over," Lizzie said. "Maybe if she meets me in a casual setting, she won't be so intimidated. She must think I'm some sort of crusader who's going to hold her captive until she submits to the Lord."

Jeffrey laughed. "I can't believe you two still haven't met."

"I haven't been very social this year, between work and wedding planning." Lizzie stretched out one leg toward Ian, grazing his arm with her big toe.

"Are you going to call her or not?" Ian asked as he grabbed Lizzie's foot and tickled it, making her laugh and twist it away from him.

Jeffrey sighed and reached for his shoes. "Not tonight. Maybe another time."

Lizzie freed her foot, gasping to catch her breath. "I don't know if we'll have much free time between now and the wedding."

"Don't worry, I won't mess up your numbers. I'll bring someone." Jeffrey stood. "I'll catch you guys later."

CHAPTER THREE

Ian closed the door behind Jeffrey then wandered into the kitchen. Empty water glasses and a couple of plates sat in the sink. The coffee pot was a quarter full, but the burner had been turned off long ago. He reached for the pot and poured the liquid down the drain then turned on the water to fill the sink.

"Leave them," Lizzie said from her place in the living room.

Ian held his hand under the faucet, testing the temperature. The house needed a new hot water heater, but he didn't want to stress Lizzie out with that. He'd deal with it after the wedding.

He watched Lizzie push herself over the arm of her chair, her bare feet making a tiny splat on the wooden floor. She padded across the room, placed her elbows on the kitchen bar and rested her chin in her hands.

"I was thinking about making some tea. Would you like some?" Ian reached for the electric kettle Lizzie kept near the sink.

Lizzie nodded and Ian dipped the kettle under the faucet. When it was half-full, he set it on the warmer and turned it on.

"Do we have any wedding plans we need to go over?" he asked.

"Probably, but I'd rather enjoy some quiet time with you."

Ian put in the drain stopper and poured dish soap into the sink, bubbles forming under the splash of the faucet.

"Leave them. I can clean up tomorrow." Lizzie reached across the bar and turned off the water.

"It will only take a minute. I can have them washed before our tea is ready." Ian turned the water back on. "Why don't you find us a movie to watch and then curl up on the couch? I'll bring your tea when it's ready. What flavor do you want?"

Lizzie titled her head and directed her gaze at the ceiling. "Pumpkin chai seems appropriate tonight."

Ian grimaced. "Haven't you had enough pumpkin today?"

Her wide eyes and gasp of horror made Ian chuckle. "There's no such thing as enough pumpkin."

"All right, my apologies." He held up his hands in surrender. "One pumpkin chai coming up."

She pushed off the bar and sauntered to a large bookcase filled with a mixture of books and DVDs. He watched her run her fingers along the spines, trying to anticipate which one she would choose. He hoped it wasn't *Ever After* again. She had a habit of quoting the lines along with the actors. When she moved past the first shelf, he turned his attention to the dishes, scrubbing them clean and setting them on a dishtowel to dry.

When the water in the kettle started boiling, Ian pulled two mugs from a cabinet and selected two tea bags from a hand-carved tea box he'd made for her birthday. He dropped the bags into the mugs and poured the boiling water over them.

"Are you sure you don't want me to ask Stephen to be one of my groomsmen?" he asked as he stirred some honey into his mug.

Lizzie sat on the floor in front of the television, loading a disc into the DVD player. "The wedding's in three weeks. It's a little late to be making changes to the wedding party."

"I know, but I'm sure Dave would understand if I asked him to step down."

Lizzie stood up, reached for the remote control and turned to face him. "You and Dave have been friends since sixth grade. Why would you replace him with someone you've only known a year?"

Ian discarded the tea bags and carried the mugs to the coffee table. "I know how close you and Stephen have gotten. It makes sense for him to be a part of the wedding."

"I thought about having him as my man-of-honor. I'm closer to him than any of the girls I know, but I didn't want him to feel awkward." Lizzie sat down on the couch, curling her legs up underneath her. "Plus, it will be nice to have him free to handle any last minute calamities that might arise."

Ian slipped an arm around her and pulled her closer. "There aren't going to be any last minute calamities."

"You haven't dealt with many weddings. There's always something that goes wrong."

"I haven't seen Dave in two years."

Lizzie reached up and placed a finger on his lips. "This isn't the time for cold feet about your groomsmen. I'm sure Dave will be fine."

She pressed the play button, the surround sound system he'd set up the previous week blared out the fanfare for *Star Wars* before he could speak again. He reached for his cup of tea and took a sip. The combination of lemon, ginger and honey had a soothing effect. He knew she was right. Dave had been his friend for years, even if they didn't stay in touch regularly, but he wasn't sure how Dave would react to seeing Jeffrey as Ian's best man.

CHAPTER FOUR

Grey skies and a brisk wind greeted the congregation as the church service ended and they all went out into the world. Children chased each other in the grass while their parents made plans to meet for lunch. Lizzie and Ian walked hand-in-hand through the crowd, weaving through the cars already lining up to leave the parking lot.

Ian held the car door open for Lizzie. "Ron and Emma are meeting us at Harvest Cafe, right?"

"Yes, as soon as Emma finishes in the nursery. Ron said we should go ahead and get a table." She ducked into the car, making sure her coat was clear of the door before Ian closed it. When he opened his own, a gust of wind howled in and she shivered.

"I hope the rain holds off until this evening." Ian put the car in reverse and waited for a line of traffic to pass before backing out of the parking spot.

"Me too. Riding in this car makes me feel like we are swimming through the puddles."

"This car is part amphibian, you know." He reached for her hand and placed it under his, on top of the gearshift.

"I'm sure that's supposed to be reassuring, but I still feel more comfortable being above the puddles instead of in them."

"I guess I'll have to get a monster truck for rainy days."

Lizzie laughed. "Jeffrey I can picture in a monster truck, but you," she laughed some more, "not so much."

Ian shifted into second as they accelerated away from the church. "That's because you haven't seen my tough side yet."

Her laughter bubbled until she could barely breathe, not stopping until they'd pulled into the café's parking lot. She regained her composure while Ian scurried around to open her door.

"I'm sorry." She accepted his hand to help her out. "I haven't laughed that hard in months."

"I'm happy I could provide you with such comic relief," he grumbled.

"Oh stop it." She playfully slapped his chest. "You know the idea of you as a rough, tough redneck is just absurd."

She saw his lips twitch and knew he was suppressing a smile. He closed the door and they walked to the restaurant. Inside, the smells of fresh bread and garlic warmed her immediately.

"My two favorite people," bellowed a burly man in his mid-fifties, with thick brown hair and deep brown eyes.

"Good afternoon, Tony." Lizzie leaned in to accept the man's kiss on each cheek.

"Is it just the two of you today?"

"No, another couple will be joining us." Ian shrugged off his coat and draped it over his arm.

"Are you talking wedding plans?" A conspiratorial gleam filled Tony's eyes.

"It's Ron and Emma so the wedding may come up," Lizzie said.

"Oh yes, the Websters, a lovely couple. Come, follow me." Tony led them to a large round table that could seat eight.

"We don't need such a big table," Lizzie protested.

Tony waved off her concerns. "You need room to spread out, to talk. This way you will have some privacy. I will send them over when they arrive."

"Thank you, Tony." Ian shook the man's hand then laid his coat in one of the chairs before turning to Lizzie. "Let me help you with your jacket."

She let Ian lift the trench coat from her shoulders. He laid it on top of his own, then pulled out a chair for her. "You make me feel like the lady of the manor."

Ian took the seat next to her and kissed her hand. "Soon you will be."

"I'd hardly call my cottage a manor."

"You can have any house you want. I'll even design you one." He winked. "Maybe I already have."

A memory tickled at the edge of Lizzie's mind, but before she could grasp it, the sound of rain battering down on the roof interrupted her thoughts. She looked out the window, the cars in the parking lot now reduced to shadows. The door opened, amplifying the sound of the rain, and Emma hurried inside, Ron close behind, his umbrella leaving a trail of water on the dark tile floor.

Tony met them and took the umbrella, placing it in a stand near the front counter, then escorted them to the table.

"What a storm." Emma used her napkin to dry off her face.

"We almost made it to the door before the bottom dropped out." Ron dropped his wet coat over the back of a chair, then took out his handkerchief and ran it over his shimmering head. "By the time I got the umbrella open, we were steps away from the awning."

Tony returned with a carafe of coffee. "I thought you could use something to warm you up."

"Thank you." Emma wrapped her hands around the cup as soon as he'd finished filling it.

"I will send a server over in a few minutes to get your orders." Tony filled the remaining cups and hurried off.

"Did you finalize the menu for the wedding?" Emma asked.

Lizzie poured some cream and two packets of sugar into her coffee. "We keep going back and forth between one or two carving stations. Does anyone want turkey when Christmas is the next week?"

"You could do chicken and roast beef instead," Emma said.

"That's what I thought, too," Ian said.

"I've never been impressed with roast beef on a buffet." Lizzie wrinkled her nose. "It always seems dry."

"What about the other items?"

"I think my favorite is the mashed potato bar. The potatoes are served in a martini glass and guests can choose to add cheese, sour cream, bacon bits, or chives. I'd be happy eating just that." Lizzie licked her lips. Mashed potatoes were her favorite comfort food and thinking about all the things she could add to them made her stomach rumble.

"We'll also have corn, green beans, macaroni salad, Caesar salad, fresh fruit, and three types of cheese," Ian said before took taking a sip of his coffee. "We just need to decide on the meat."

Lizzie shrugged. "If you all think roast beef is the way to go, then I'm fine with that. Who knows if I'll even have time to eat. None of the bridal magazines I've read mention anything about the bride eating. There are tips on make-up, dancing, decorating, how to carry the flowers, gifts for the wedding party, emergency supply kits, even how to get the flower girl and ring bearers to behave, but nothing about how to eat elegantly."

Ron chuckled. "I don't think Emma ate anything other than the piece of cake I gave her; she was so busy talking to everyone." He patted his stomach. "I, on the other hand, ate every chance I got. My best man would bring me a little plate every ten minutes or so."

"I'll have to make sure Jeffrey's on top of that," Ian said.

A server appeared, placing a basket of fresh bread on the table before taking their orders. Ian reached for the basket, snatched a piece of bread and passed it on. They then all focused on buttering the warm bread and enjoying their first bites.

CHAPTER FIVE

"What flavor cake did you choose?" Emma said breaking the silence.

Lizzie popped the last bit of bread into her mouth and chewed slowly. Most of the wedding planning had gone well. She'd made lots of contacts through her work at the hotel. Flowers had been the easiest. One call to her friend Jackson at Fields of Bloom and twenty minutes later all the floral décor, bouquets, and boutonnieres had been decided.

The church they attended was massive, but when Pastor Donovan showed them the original chapel the campus had grown from, she fell in love. It had been restored as a prayer chapel and had grown in popularity as a wedding venue for couples looking for a more intimate ceremony.

The dress had been a bit more difficult; there were so many beautiful choices, but two days of intense shopping, trying on more than fifty gowns, and she'd found the perfect one. Food had been her downfall, though.

"We are meeting with Chef Gustave to discuss flavors tomorrow." Ian's eyes met Lizzie's and she quickly swallowed her bread.

"I wish we could have a fifteen layer cake with different flavors in each."

"Cutting it a bit close aren't you?" Emma stared at Lizzie, but she only looked down at her plate.

"Red velvet seems the logical choice, to me," Ian said. "It's a Christmassy kind of cake; we both love it, so I don't see why we need to do a tasting. Of course, I'm not going to turn down a chance to eat as much cake as I want."

Lizzie smiled. "Is that why you haven't mentioned red velvet before? So you can have a tasting?"

"The cake tasting is the best part of the planning for a guy. I shouldn't be cheated out of that, should I?" He looked at Lizzie with puppy dog eyes, and she choked on the water she was sipping.

The server returned to the table with their meals but Lizzie was still coughing and sputtering. "Oh my, what can I do?" the server fretted.

"I'm okay," Lizzie managed to say between gasps. She dabbed at her mouth with her napkin as her breathing returned to normal.

The server distributed their plates, hovering at Lizzie's elbow for another minute.

"Could I have some fresh ground pepper?" Ron asked him.

The server looked at Lizzie again, then moved around the table to grind pepper onto Ron's plate of grilled salmon.

"Thank you, that's good," Ron said as he held up his hand.

"Anyone else?" the server asked.

They all shook their heads and the server slipped away.

"That poor guy thought he was going to have to give you the Heimlich," Ron said.

"It's Ian's fault."

"What did I do?" Ian protested.

His attempt to look innocent made Lizzie smile. "Nothing, dear, nothing at all."

She reached for her fork and broke off a piece of mahi-mahi fillet. The meat melted in her mouth and she wondered if she'd made a mistake not offering fish on the wedding buffet. Of course, not everyone loved seafood as much as she did, and there was a knack to serving it well.

"What do you think?" Ian said, touching her shoulder.

"What? I'm sorry, I wasn't listening."

"Ron was asking if we would like to go to a movie this afternoon." Ian studied her and she could see the questions in his eyes.

"Sure, if we aren't out too late."

"There's a matinee showing at two thirty." Ron glanced toward the window. "It looks like the rain is letting up, so it shouldn't be a bad drive to the theater."

"That sounds fine." Lizzie speared her fish.

Ian leaned close and whispered in her ear. "You okay?"

She nodded and took another bite of her meal.

CHAPTER SIX

A golden sunset greeted the two couples when they emerged from the movie theater. Lizzie held up a hand to shield her eyes. The only evidence of the earlier downpour was a few puddles in the shadow of the theater.

"Joaquin Phoenix was rather convincing," Ron said as they crossed into the parking lot.

"He's not quite as attractive as his brother was, but he is a good actor," Emma agreed. "What did you think, Lizzie?"

"It was a good movie," she replied. "Thanks for inviting us."

Emma scrutinized her. "Are you feeling all right?"

"A bit of a headache. Nothing a good night's sleep won't cure."

Ian squeezed her hand and she knew he was concerned as well. "I think I have some Aspirin in the car. Should I go back and get you something to drink from the theater?"

They were five rows into the parking lot and closer to the car than the theater. "No, I'm fine. I'll take something when I get home."

"It's this crazy weather," Emma said. "Changes in the barometric pressure can cause headaches."

They reached Ian's BMW and stopped. Lizzie felt like she was supposed to say something, but her mind was blank. The headache had increased with each step and she could think of little more than crawling into bed.

"I hope the cake tasting goes well," Emma finally said. Ron smiled and Ian gave a small laugh.

"Red velvet does sound like a good idea," Lizzie said.

"We're still going to taste the other flavors, though, aren't we?" Ian looked down at her with a grin.

Lizzie looked up and felt the ground shift beneath her, then Ian caught her.

"Are you okay?" he asked. One hand brushed hair from her face, while the other supported her as if she weighed no more than a newspaper.

"I think I need to lie down," she said.

"Ron, can you open the door for me?" Ian dug his keys from his pocket and handed them to Ron who hurried to open the passenger door. Ian picked her up and carried her the last few steps, carefully settling her in the seat.

"Do you want us to follow you?" Emma asked.

"No, I'll be fine," Lizzie mumbled.

"I'll call you if she gets any worse." Ian closed the door and the conversation became muffled.

Lizzie closed her eyes, the pain in her head easing slightly, but she felt cold. She pulled her jacket tighter around her and stuffed her hands into its deep pockets. I can't be getting sick, she thought.

The driver's door opened and Ian slipped inside. He pressed his hand to her forehead. "I think you have a fever."

"No, I'm just tired. I shouldn't have gone to work yesterday, but there was so much to catch up on after taking Thanksgiving off."

"I don't know; the flu's been going around."

"I don't have time to be sick."

Ian pulled onto the highway. "We'll get you home and see how you feel in the morning."

Lizzie leaned her head against the window, the sound of the engine lulling her to sleep. Ian's hand on her shoulder woke her when they arrived at her house. She moved to open her door.

"I'll get it," Ian said. "I wanted to wake you up first, so you wouldn't tumble out when I did. Why don't you give me your house key now so you don't have to search for it when we get to the porch?"

Lizzie reached for her purse on the floor, but leaning forward made her stomach churn. "I don't think I can."

Ian leaned over and grabbed the bag, setting it on her lap. "The keys should be in the pocket on the left side," Lizzie said.

Ian hesitated. "Are you sure? Guys aren't supposed to go into a lady's purse."

Lizzie gave him a weak smile. "You're going to know all my secrets soon enough, you might as well brave the depths of my handbag."

Ian tugged on the zipper and dipped his hand into the bag, keeping his eyes on Lizzie. She wanted to laugh, but her headache was back. She closed her eyes.

"Found them."

"I knew you would."

She heard him open his door, the leather seat squeaking as he slid out. A few seconds later and her own door opened; she felt his hands slip under her legs and around her shoulders. She leaned into him, wrapping one arm around his neck.

"I can probably walk," she murmured.

"It's good practice for our wedding," he replied, carrying her up the steps. "I'm going to have to put you down to unlock the door."

"Okay, but put me close to the wall." Lizzie reached for the doorframe as he set her down. Her feet felt unsteady, but she had the support of the house behind her.

Ian fumbled with the keychain, half a dozen keys all looking the same. "It's the one with the yellow sticker," she said.

Finding it, he unlocked the door and moved to pick her up again.

"Carrying me over the threshold is for the wedding night. I can walk." She clutched his arm and they moved slowly through the front door.

"Do you want to go to the couch or to your bed?"

"Bed, please." She tried to remember if she'd made her bed before leaving for church and wondered if there were any clothes lying on the floor.

They staggered down the hall into the bedroom. The bed wasn't made, but other than that the room wasn't too bad. She sat down on her bed and kicked off her shoes.

"Let me help you with your jacket," Ian said, reaching for the large buttons.

"Leave it on. I'm so cold." She lay back and pulled the covers over her.

"Where's your thermometer?"

"In the bathroom somewhere."

"I love you, but I'm not ready to explore your bathroom yet. I'm pretty sure you have a fever. I'm going to make you some tea and get some Aspirin from my car."

Lizzie smiled. "I didn't know you were so scared of women."

"My mother taught me to respect a woman's purse and her medicine cabinet. She didn't tell me at what point in life those rules ended."

"Maybe you should call her and ask her."

"If you can find humor in this then I know you aren't dying. I'll be right back."

Lizzie watched him bolt from the room, then snuggled down deeper into the covers. Her feet were still cold, but the rest of her was starting to warm up. She heard the front door open and close then counted off the seconds it took for him to get to his car and find the Aspirin before the door opened and closed again. His dress shoes made a hollow clomping sound on the hardwood floor as he went into the kitchen.

When she heard him coming down the hall, she made herself sit up, propping a pillow behind herself. She squinted against the light coming through the large window. She'd always enjoyed waking to natural light and so only had thin curtains, just to keep out prying eyes. Now she wished she'd chosen thick velvet.

"I made you lemon ginger tea." He handed her the mug. "Ginger is supposed to be good for an upset stomach."

"How did you know my stomach was sick?"

"You got a little green when you tried to pick up your purse." He handed her two white tablets.

She took the pills and swallowed, carefully washing them down with the hot tea. "Would you mind bringing me a pair of socks?"

Ian looked toward the dresser then back at her.

"They have their own drawer; you won't see anything unmentionable. Not that I have any exciting unmentionables. Top right drawer."

He moved to the dresser, took a deep breath, and opened the drawer. He pulled out a pair of fuzzy pink socks and held them up.

"Those are perfect." Lizzie pushed the comforter and blanket back, took the socks, and put them on her icy feet. She unbuttoned her jacket and slipped it off, allowing it to drop onto the floor, before she burrowed back into the bed.

"Is the tea helping to warm you up?" Ian asked. Lizzie nodded. "What else can I get for you?"

"In the window seat, there are a couple of extra blankets. Would you mind hanging one over the curtain rod? The light is making my headache worse."

"I can do that." Ian lifted the window seat lid and chose a navy blue blanket. Closing the lid, he stood on the seat and tucked several inches of the blanket over the curtain rod, making sure to cover as much of the window as possible.

Lizzie felt instant relief. "Thank you. That's much better."

"Do you want me to call Emma?"

"You can let her know I'm okay; there's nothing she can do. If it is the flu, I don't want to give it to her."

"I designed a medical complex a couple of years ago. I got to know several of the doctors and they told me if I ever needed anything to give them a call. I could see if one of them could come over."

Lizzie reached out to him and he moved closer to the bed. She took his hand. "That isn't necessary. If I don't feel better tomorrow, I'll go to the doctor. I just want to finish my tea and go to sleep. You should go home."

Ian sat down on the edge of the bed. "I'm going to stay here until you fall asleep."

"At least let me finish my tea." She reached for the cup on her bedside table.

When she'd drained the last drop and returned the cup to the table, he pulled the blankets up around her shoulders and tucked her in. "Close your eyes now and sleep."

She met his gaze for a moment but then closed her eyes.

CHAPTER SEVEN

Her breathing grew steady, her face relaxed, and her grip on the top of her blanket loosened. Ian sat and watched, longing to caress the face he loved so dearly, but feared waking her. He eased off the bed, collected her empty cup, and pulled the door partially closed behind him.

The house was quiet without Lizzie's laughter. It reminded him of the nights he'd worked alone here to refinish the floors, and the moment she'd first seen the finished product. Even speckled with paint and her hair tangled she'd been beautiful.

In the kitchen, he opened the refrigerator and reached for some Thanksgiving leftovers, then drew back his hand, wondering if any of it had been responsible for Lizzie's illness. With a shrug, he filled a plate and popped it into the microwave. When the meal was ready, he grabbed a soda and went to the living room. He flipped through a wedding magazine on the coffee table as he ate, smiling at the pages Lizzie had folded over. An article about honeymoon planning made him think of Stephen and he pulled his cell phone from his pocket.

"Hey, Stephen, it's Ian."

"Hi."

"I don't think Lizzie's going to make it to the office tomorrow. I think she has the flu."

"Oh, man, that's not good."

"Stephen, are you all right? You don't sound so good yourself."

"I've got a nasty headache. It started about an hour ago."

"Uh oh," Ian said and stretched out on the couch. "That's how it started with Lizzie."

"We can't both be sick."

"Sorry to be the bearer of bad news." The sound of breaking glass jolted Ian upright. "I gotta go. I hope you feel better."

Ian dropped his cell phone on the couch and ran down the hall. In Lizzie's bedroom, he found the bedside lamp on the floor, glass from the broken bulb scattered everywhere. He looked at the bed, but Lizzie wasn't there. He picked his way through the debris to the bathroom where he could hear her retching.

"I'm here, baby," he whispered, kneeling down behind her and tenderly gathering her hair back away from her face.

She whimpered, then heaved again. He saw a scrunchie on the vanity and reached for it, securing her hair at the nape of her neck. He rubbed her back and when the heaving stopped, pulled her into his lap.

"Do you feel better?" he asked.

"I don't know," Lizzie croaked.

"Let me get you back to bed." Ian moved to stand.

Lizzie put a hand on his shoulder. "Not yet."

He leaned back against the vanity, holding her close to his chest. "We'll stay here as long as you need to."

"What time is it?"

He had to check his watch. "Six fifteen."

"Thank you for staying."

"Of course I stayed. I wouldn't leave you alone like this." He buried his face in her hair.

"I think I can move now." Lizzie stirred from his lap, placing her hands on the floor, trying to push herself up.

Ian stood and scooped her up, carrying her to her bed. She still had on the long skirt and sweater she'd worn to church. "Do you want me to get you some pajamas to change into?"

"I don't have the energy to change." She looked down at her clothes. "These aren't so bad. I could use something to drink, though."

He fluffed her pillows and helped her pull the blankets up. "I'll be right back."

In the kitchen, he grabbed a can of soda, then debated pouring it into a glass, but opted not to. At the last minute, he opened the small pantry and took out a broom.

"Here you go," he said, popping the tab on the drink and handing her the can, then picked up the lamp and started sweeping up the broken glass.

"I'm sorry. I was so desperate to get to the bathroom I must have knocked that over."

"It's okay." With the glass swept into a pile, Ian went into the bathroom and found a washcloth. He came back and placed the dampened cloth on Lizzie's forehead. He noticed her eyes were bright and pressed the back of his hand against her cheek.

"You're fever's worse."

"I don't think I'm going to work tomorrow."

"I already called Stephen," Ian assured her. He wasn't going to worry her with the possibility that Stephen was sick also. She'd drag herself into the office carrying a bucket if she thought both of them were going to be out.

"What about the cake? We have to make a decision." She struggled to sit up and Ian gently pressed her shoulder's back down.

"Don't worry about that now. Rest." He removed the washcloth and took it back to the bathroom, running cold water over it. When he returned to place it on her forehead again, her eyes were closed.

"I'm not asleep," she said.

He leaned down and ran the cloth over her face and neck. A memory of his mother doing the same thing for him as a child flashed into his mind.

"I promise not to get sick like this after we're married," Lizzie murmured.

Ian ran the cloth around her hairline. "For better or for worse; I made that vow the day I bought your engagement ring. I don't need a ceremony to make me stand by it."

Lizzie reached for his hand and pulled it to her lips. "I love you."

"I love you, too. Now go back to sleep."

CHAPTER EIGHT

Ian jolted from a deep sleep, woken by the wail of a passing police siren. He looked around, not recognizing his surroundings, but then he heard a toilet flush and everything came into focus. He threw back the comforter and reached for his pants draped over the back of a chair. Crossing the hall from the guest bedroom to the master, he found Lizzie's bed empty and the bathroom door closed.

He knocked on it. "Are you okay?"

The door flew open and Lizzie stepped back in surprise. She'd changed into a pair of sweatpants and a baggy t-shirt.

"What are you doing here?" she asked.

"I stayed in the guest bedroom. I was afraid you might need something during the night. You look better."

Lizzie touched her hair, which she'd brushed and pulled back in a ponytail. "I look awful."

"You should have seen yourself last night, hunched over the toilet."

"That wasn't a nightmare?" She covered her face with both her hands, shaking her head.

"It probably felt like one, but it was real. After the second round of throwing up you seemed to feel better."

"What time was that?"

"About one this morning." Ian glanced at his watch. "I better call Sheila and tell her I'm working from home today."

"You don't have to do that. I feel better."

"I don't have any clients coming in today. I'll run home, change clothes, and grab my computer."

"I'm a little weak, but I'll be fine." Lizzie stepped out of the bathroom and made her way to her bed.

"I'm sure you're right, but I don't want to risk exposing Sheila. The office can't run without her."

Lizzie turned with a look of distress. "You aren't sick now, are you?"

"I don't think so, but better to be safe, though." He straightened her blankets and patted the mattress. "Climb in. I'll bring you some toast to try."

Lizzie scrunched up her face at the mention of food as she climbed into bed. "I don't know if I'm ready for toast yet."

"Then something to drink. You need to stay hydrated. I'll bring you some water and a soda. Then when I come back you can try some food."

"Okay." She leaned back against the pillows and he could tell the effort of cleaning up had left her drained.

Ian hurried to get her settled with beverages and a pile of magazines. "If you get tired before I get back, go to sleep. I'll take your keys with me and let myself back in."

On the way to his condo, he called to update Emma and assure her that everything was under control. He also called Stephen, but only got his voicemail.

"I hope the kid is okay," Ian muttered after cancelling the call, then he dialed his office as he pulled into the lot for his condo.

"Mr. Canvanaugh, are you all right?" Sheila answered on the first ring.

"I'm fine, Sheila. Lizzie has the flu. I'm going to work from home today to make sure she is okay."

"The poor thing. It's going around something fierce. How are you feeling?"

"Tired, but I can catch up on sleep."

"If you need anything you give me a call."

"Thanks, Sheila. You can forward the office phone to my cell and go home if you'd like."

"There are some invoices I need to take care of, but I may leave early. I'll let you know."

Ian ended the call and stuffed the phone in his pocket as he stepped on the elevator, pushing the button for the fifth floor. Once inside his apartment, he made a beeline for the bedroom where he pulled a pair of jeans and a light, long-sleeve shirt from the closet. He didn't want to leave

Lizzie alone any longer than necessary, but he now felt covered in germs and couldn't resist a hot shower.

Half an hour later, he closed the front door behind him. A duffel bag with a change of clothes was slung over one shoulder and a messenger bag with his laptop and some files hung from the other. He didn't wait for the elevator, but hurried down the stairs to the parking lot.

Not a cloud blemished the cerulean sky and he decided to open the sunroof. It wasn't often Florida presented such a gorgeous day. The temperature was a perfect seventy-two degrees, with minimal wind. He arrived back at Lizzie's, his hair dried from the drive. When he turned the key, he nudged the door open, trying to be as quiet as possible in case she'd fallen back asleep.

"No need to be quiet, I'm awake," Lizzie called down the hall.

He stopped in the guest room to drop his bags then crossed the hall. "How are you feeling?"

Lizzie closed the magazine she'd been reading. "Still woozy when I try to get up, but I haven't tossed anymore cookies."

"That's good to hear. You ready for some toast?"

"I think so. Do you know where my cell phone is?"

"No, my guess is it's in your purse. Why?"

"I want to call Stephen, make sure everything's okay at work."

Ian shook his head. "Wrong answer. You aren't going to worry about work. They can do without you for one day."

"What if something comes up and they need to ask me a question?"

"You've taught Stephen everything you know. He's more than capable of handling things. He held down the fort while you went on vacation in February; he'll do fine now."

Lizzie started to protest, but Ian held up his hand and shook his head. She closed her mouth and reached for her magazine again.

"I'll be back with your toast in a few minutes."

In the kitchen, Ian turned on the kettle, and placed two pieces of bread in the toaster. His stomach growled, reminding him how long it had been since he'd eaten. He found a bowl and filled it with cereal. Before he could pour any milk in, the toast popped up and the kettle started boiling.

"Your toast and some tea," he announced as he entered the bedroom a few minutes later.

Lizzie sat up, propping a couple of pillows behind her back. "Have you eaten anything?"

"I have a bowl of cereal waiting for me."

"And you're still feeling okay?"

"I'm fine. Takes more than a little flu bug to get me down."

Lizzie smiled. "Is this the tough side you were telling me about?"

"Maybe." He sat down on the end of the bed. "Do you like it?"

She laughed. "Too early to tell."

He sighed and stood up. "Is there anything else I can get for you?"

She shook her head. "Not right now."

"All right. I'm going to check some emails then." He kissed her forehead, collected his laptop from the guest bedroom and his cereal from the kitchen, and settled in at the dining room table.

CHAPTER NINE

Stephen sat at his desk, his head in his hands, hoping the world would stop spinning.

"You don't look so good."

He glanced up to find Ben, one of the concierge team members, standing over him. "I don't feel so good."

"Why didn't you stay home, then?"

"Because Lizzie's out sick."

"I thought she was down in the group office trying to straighten out that new guy; what's his name?"

"Melvin Sinclair. His attention span is worse than yours."

"Hey, I don't have a problem with paying attention. So Lizzie's sick, too. Were you two fooling around?" Ben gave Stephen a mischievous look.

"Of course not." Stephen had tried to sound indignant, but raising his voice made his headache worse. "Don't you have some work to do?"

"Oh, yeah, that's why I was coming to see you. Elaine Henderson is scheduled to check in this afternoon, but I couldn't find a welcome packet for her."

Stephen groaned. "Of all the days for her to arrive."

Elaine was a regular at the resort, coming for a visit every six to eight weeks. She was the first concierge guest Stephen had taken over from Lizzie the previous year, and she was a handful.

Every time she checked-in she had specific requests for her room and required a formal itinerary for each day of her stay. She always traveled alone and Stephen had never figured out why she stayed with them so often. He pulled his keyboard closer and started typing.

"I'll print up her itinerary. She doesn't get a regular welcome packet." He pointed to his bottom desk drawer. "I have special folders for her in there. Would you mind grabbing one, please?"

Ben opened the drawer and thumbed through several hanging files. "Is this it?"

Stephen glanced at the folder Ben held up. "Yes. All you need to do is add her itinerary. Do you think you're ready to handle her check-in?"

"Sure, no problem."

Stephen stopped typing and looked at Ben. "You know who Elaine is, right?"

"She's been here a few times."

"She's been here thirty-seven times in the past two years alone."

"Why does she come here so much?"

"I have no idea, but she is very demanding. Speaking of which, make sure we have a bottle of Santa Margherita Pinot Grigio chilling in the lounge. She'll want a glass as soon as she's checked in."

"Are you sure you don't want to take care of her?" Ben sat in a chair across from Stephen.

"It's time for you and Jessica to start taking care of some of the frequent fliers."

"She's not the only one?"

"I wish she were, but there are about ten others. We'll talk about them later." Stephen returned his attention to the computer. "Today, you take care of Elaine."

The printer clacked and whined, then rolled out two pages. Stephen pointed at it. "There's her itinerary. Memorize it because she will ask questions during her stay. When she asks for me or Lizzie, tell her we're out sick, but you are prepared to assist her."

Stephen reached for a box of index cards, flipped through them until he found the one he wanted and handed it to Ben. "Here are the important details you need to know about her."

Ben took the card. "I don't know about this."

"You've been here a year, you should have been dealing with these guests a long time ago. Now pull yourself together. Elaine will eat you alive if she senses you are nervous." Stephen stopped talking and reached for the garbage can under his desk. A violent shudder ran through him as his stomach turned inside out, forcing its contents into the can.

This happened twice more before he caught his breath. He rested his forehead on the desk, the can held between his knees a foot away from his face. With one hand he felt along the desk top for a napkin or a tissue. A roll of paper towels was shoved into his view, which he grabbed, tearing off several to wipe off his face.

"You should go home," Ben said, his own voice shaky.

"No, I feel better now," Stephen lied. He dropped the dirty paper towels into the garbage can and pulled the bag free, tying it closed. "Would you call housekeeping, please?"

Ben didn't respond, but moved several feet away to another desk where Stephen could hear him dialing the phone and talking to the housekeeping manager.

A few minutes later one of the housekeepers came in with a large garbage can. She made her way to Stephen's desk and took the bag from the can, replacing it with a fresh one. She patted him on the shoulder and pulled a can of Coke from her apron pocket.

"I thought you might need this," she said as she set it on the desk.

"Thank you, Amelia."

Stephen opened it and took a tentative sip before taking a long drink. He checked the clock on his computer. It was only noon; four more hours to go.

CHAPTER TEN

Jeffrey sat at his desk, using a pen to drum a monotonous rhythm while he studied the calendar in front of him. He had a little more than two weeks to find a date for Lizzie and Ian's wedding. He couldn't ask just anyone; weddings were events that made women sentimental. If a guy invited one to a wedding he was sending a message that he was interested in a serious relationship. He wasn't ready to be serious with anyone and Lizzie was the only female friend he would consider taking to such an event.

"You're going to beat a hole in that desk if you don't stop that."

Jeffrey swiveled his chair. Jenny, his officer manager, glared at him from her desk across the small trailer.

"Sorry."

"What's bothering you? Construction is back on schedule; we're on target for completion in the spring."

"Thank goodness for a quiet hurricane season this year."

"So if it's not work, what is it?"

"I told Lizzie I'd have a date for the wedding, but I don't."

"What about Michelle?"

"Doesn't that send the wrong message?"

"Have you done anything to lead her to believe you're more than just friends?"

Jeffrey shrugged. "I don't think so."

"Then be honest. Tell her you need a plus one and she's your only female friend."

"She's not my only female friend." He leaned forward. "What about you? Would you like to go with me?"

Jenny rolled her eyes. "No, thanks."

"Why not? It could be fun."

"You're my boss. A great boss and all, but I don't mix work with my personal life."

Jeffrey thought a moment, realizing he didn't know much about Jenny other than what happened at work. "Fair enough. I should probably keep my personal life out of my work."

"That would take all the fun out of my day." Jenny chuckled. "Hearing about your mess of a life has made this job bearable."

"I have turned into a moaning Nelly, haven't I? Good grief." Jeffrey stood up and moved to the coffee pot. The liquid smelled burned, but he poured a cup anyway, adding four packets of sugar to cover the bitterness.

"Can I say something without it reflecting on me as your employee?"

"I'm not going to like what you say, am I?"

"Probably not, but I only have your best interests at heart."

Jeffrey nodded. "Go ahead."

"You're a good guy, even more so since the scaffolding accident last summer. Granted you were a wreck at the time, but something changed in you a few weeks later. I've heard you talking to Wally about church and I gather you've been going." She paused and shuffled some papers on her desk.

"Yeah, I found religion," Jeffrey said wryly.

Jenny looked up and met his gaze. "You make it sound like a bad thing. I don't think you just found religion, lots of people say that but their actions don't change. You don't come in reeking of alcohol, you are more compassionate, and I saw the struggle you went through when you had to let the original plumbers go. You have changed, and for the better."

Jeffrey set down the empty coffee cup. "But…"

"But you seem more isolated. You don't go out with the guys after work. The only people you ever talk about are Michelle, Lizzie, and Ian. Have you made any other new friends to go along with this new life you seem to be leading?"

"I have gotten to be pretty good friends with Stephen, one of the guys Lizzie works with."

"So, you've downsized your social circle from dozens of friends to four."

"I wouldn't say I had dozens of friends before. Acquaintances, sure, I had plenty of those, but few people I could depend on."

Jenny nodded. "You do need to have people you can depend on, but you need other people too. You need a social circle that shares your values, to show you how to have fun in this new life."

Jeffrey thought about the countless nights he'd sat home alone, unable to think of a way to entertain himself that didn't involve drinking, gambling, or women. He'd given those things up the previous year, but they were still his only point of reference. It was this struggle that had made him call Stephen a few times, until they'd become friends, almost by default.

"I haven't upset you, have I?" Jenny fidgeted with a ring on her right hand, turning it round and round.

Jeffrey closed his eyes and blew out a loud breath. "No, this isn't even the first time I've been told I'm isolating myself. If you see it too, then it's likely true."

When he looked at Jenny again, she had stopped fidgeting and looked relieved. "I've heard you talking to Wally about a group at your church you think he should get involved in. Are you a part of that group?"

"No, it's a group for single parents."

"Aren't there other groups you could be part of?"

"Yeah, there are, and if I ever want Wally to come around, I may need to take my own advice." Jeffrey shook his head.

He'd met Wally when he'd taken on the project manager job for this construction site two years previously. They'd hit it off and had started hitting the bars together every weekend. After Jeffrey bottomed out and came to know God, he'd tried to share his new faith with Wally, who'd been dealt a tough hand but he didn't want to hear it.

Wally had married his high school sweetheart; they'd had a child together and been a happy family. When their son, Tim, was only five, she died. Nine years had passed, but Wally was still bitter.

"That still doesn't solve my problem of a date for the wedding." Jeffrey returned to his chair and slumped down.

"Talk to Michelle. She seems to be your only option."

CHAPTER ELEVEN

Cubicle walls stretched as far as the eye could see. The tan cloth and bare metal reminded Michelle of a desert landscape. She walked down the long hallway to the break room, an oasis of activity at this hour.

In contrast to all the tan cubicles, this was a relaxing arctic blue. The appliances were stainless steel, and gleaming in the bright fluorescent light. Three wooden tables, in a warm espresso tone, filled one corner of the room, a pair of vending machines another.

"Hey, Wendy. What's for lunch?" Michelle asked as she pulled her own thermal bag out of the refrigerator.

A young woman with thick brown hair and bold make-up, which made her brown eyes appear enormous, was already seated at one of the tables, a plastic take-out container in front of her.

"Leftovers from dinner at PF Chang," Wendy said.

"That sounds better than my tuna sandwich. Want to trade?"

"No way." Wendy scooped up a large helping of rice.

"How was your Thanksgiving?"

"Nothing exciting. You?"

Michelle pulled her sandwich from a Ziploc baggie. "Spent the day with my parents and some cousins who were in town."

"You didn't talk to Jeffrey?"

Michelle took a bite of her sandwich and shrugged.

"You can call him, you know."

"I do, sometimes."

"Why are you so dead set on making this difficult?"

"I don't know what you mean."

Wendy set down her fork and waited until Michelle looked at her. "You like the guy. You aren't dating anyone else. Why don't you get serious about him?"

"Jeffrey and I aren't dating."

"Sure, keep telling yourself that."

"We aren't," Michelle insisted. "We haven't even talked in two weeks."

"So, are you dating someone I don't know about?"

Michelle took another bite of her sandwich.

"I'll take that as a no. You aren't getting any younger and he seems like a really nice guy. What's the problem?"

"I've told you. He wants me to go to church and believe in Jesus."

"You *have* been going to church."

Michelle dropped the remaining half of her sandwich. "How do you know that?"

"I saw you leaving a few weeks ago. I was meeting a friend who goes there. I asked her and she said she'd seen you almost every week for the past three months."

"As big as this city is and it's still too small to keep anything a secret," Michelle grumbled.

"Why does it need to be a secret?"

"I need to figure this out for myself. Jeffrey is very convincing. I know how much his life has changed since he became a believer, but I need to see all the angles."

"Have you figured anything out?"

Michelle opened a bag of chips and nibbled on one as she thought. Finding the body of her coworker, Amanda, earlier in the year, had awoken in her a desire to understand God. In addition to attending church services, she'd been doing research online, and had even talked to a shrink about the existence of God.

"There's enough evidence outside the Bible to make me believe there was a guy named Jesus who was well respected and reviled equally. There are historical accounts of many of his followers continuing to preach of his death and resurrection, despite the persecution they faced, even to the point of their own deaths."

"Not many people have that kind of faith today," Wendy said.

"I wouldn't say that. We just don't hear about it as often. Online there are numerous accounts of people in other countries speaking of miracles they've witnessed and proclaiming them to be works of God. Even when they are threatened they don't back down."

"So, does that mean you're a believer?"

Michelle stood up and went to the water cooler, filling a large bottle. "There are still so many questions, like how could God have allowed Amanda to be killed? She wasn't my favorite person by any means, but she wasn't a bad person."

Wendy nodded. "Questions like that are some of the biggest hurdles on the road to belief. Even people who've been Christians for years struggle to understand the reason why some things happen."

"How do you overcome those hurdles then?"

"Faith. It all comes down to the free will God gave us. Some people are going to use that freedom to do evil things. We are all given choices, to do good or to do bad. Maybe the definition of good and bad is different for some people. I don't know since I've never known anyone truly evil."

"You and I don't have different definitions. Heck, I didn't even know you believed in God until this conversation."

Wendy shrugged. "I admit I let my faith slide, but since Amanda's death I've been rethinking things. I got back into church over the summer and I'm starting to see things more clearly."

"I wish I could see clearly. I feel like as soon as I untangle one mystery, I open the door to another."

"That's part of faith, believing in things we can't see, or even understand. How can we possibly understand unconditional love like God offers us? We have all kinds of conditions we place on our love. We don't love those who don't love us in return. We don't love those who commit terrible acts. We don't love the guy on the highway who cuts us off in rush hour traffic."

Michelle thought about this, knowing there were many people in her past she couldn't even begin to offer her love to. They'd hurt her too badly for her to open her heart to them again.

Wendy speared a piece of chicken and popped it into her mouth. When she'd swallowed, she said, "You should talk to Jeffrey, let him know what you've been doing. He's still new to faith and I'm sure he's had some of the same questions. Ask him what answers he's found."

Michelle nodded. "Maybe you're right."

"Of course I am." Wendy smiled. "When am I ever wrong?"

Michelle laughed. "Nice to see you're still humble."

"I try to keep myself grounded. It can be hard sometimes, being as awesome as I am."

CHAPTER TWELVE

Ian looked up from his laptop to see Lizzie in the doorway of the den, a thick bathrobe wrapped around her. As he set his laptop on a side table and stood up, he marveled at how her pale face made her blue eyes more brilliant than ever.

"How are you feeling?"

"A little better."

"What can I do for you?"

"I needed to get out of bed. Do you know where my cell phone is?"

Ian patted his pocket. "No one has called."

She held her hand out. "I should check on Stephen."

Ian shook his head. "You know he will call if he needs you."

"Not if he knows I'm sick."

"That's just as well. You aren't in any condition to do anything to help him."

Lizzie dropped her hand and leaned against the doorframe. "I know you're right, but I feel awful leaving him alone."

"He's not alone. Ben and Jessica are working today, right?"

"Yeah, but…"

"But, nothing," and Ian reached for her hand. "You aren't the only one who can get the job done."

He took her hand and pulled her into the room, guiding her to the chair he'd been sitting in. When she was seated, he touched her forehead, relieved to find it was cool to the touch.

"What time is it?" she asked.

"Almost two-thirty. You had a good nap."

"I'm still so tired." She slumped back in the chair and closed her eyes.

"Would you like to try to eat something before lying down again?"

She only shrugged. Ian looked down at her; she looked so small in the large wing-backed chair. "How about some crackers and tea?"

"That's fine," she whispered.

"Do you want to stay in here or go back to your room?"

She opened her eyes and moved to stand up. "I think I want to lie on the couch for a while."

She got to her feet and Ian slipped a supporting arm around her waist. He gave her a minute to gain her balance, then matched her steps until they'd reached the living room. He helped her onto the couch and handed her the television remote control.

"I can't remember the last time I watched daytime TV," she said.

"I don't think much has changed." Ian crossed to the kitchen and turned on the kettle before rummaging through cabinets looking for crackers. By the time he'd found them, the water was boiling. He allowed the tea to steep for a couple of minutes, watching as Lizzie flipped through the channels, barely taking time to see what was on.

"I could put a movie in for you," he offered as he set the plate and cup of tea on the coffee table.

"That's okay." She punched in a channel number and the picture changed to a home improvement show.

Ian moaned. "No more DIY projects, please."

Lizzie smiled, looking more like her old self. "Don't worry. I don't have any more plans, not for a few months anyway."

"I talked with Chef Gustave earlier and he said we could move the cake tasting to Friday."

"You called Chef?" Lizzie struggled to sit up.

"He wasn't as scary as you've made him out. When I told him you were sick he insisted we wait until you are better."

"He's not scary, he's more…" her gaze roamed the room, "particular."

Ian grinned. "And he particularly told me to make sure you get better soon."

"I'm sure he did. He doesn't like the new group manager."

"Why not?"

Lizzie sighed and stretched out on the couch. "Melvin has the shortest attention span of anyone I've ever met. He gets distracted by every noise in the hallway, every person walking by, it's like he can't focus on any single thing. Every time he has to talk to Chef about a menu, it takes half an hour."

"I can see how that would be annoying. How'd he get the job in the first place?"

She shrugged. "The fact he's lasted two months is mystifying."

"Well, I hope he lasts another two so we can have our wedding and honeymoon without you worrying about the hotel." Ian brushed a stray hair off her forehead and tucked it behind her ear.

She frowned. "I've thought about asking Stephen if he'd be interested in the job. I feel terrible that he's been in limbo for so long. When he was offered the human resources job in the spring, I was sure he wanted it. We all thought Tammy would return to the group office in a couple of weeks and everything would go back to normal. He would then have been free to make the move to HR."

"Has he mentioned being unhappy about staying?"

"No, but he wouldn't."

Ian nodded. "He looks up to you, you know, and wants to make you proud of him."

"I am proud of him. He's grown so much in the past year." She met Ian's gaze. "I wonder if I tell him enough what a good job he does."

He could see concern in her eyes and searched for the words to ease her mind. He leaned forward and clasped his hands in front of his knees. "I'm sure he knows how much you appreciate him. I don't think he would work so hard if he didn't."

She seemed to consider this for a long time. "I hope you're right."

The phone in Ian's pocket rang. He recognized the song as Emma's ringtone and handed the phone to Lizzie.

"Hi, Emma."

Ian went to the kitchen to make himself a snack, catching only Lizzie's side of the conversation. He'd given Emma an update that morning, but wasn't surprised the woman was calling to check-in. The bond between Emma and Lizzie was almost as close as between mother and daughter.

He was grateful Lizzie had Emma and Ron in her life to help fill the gap left by her parents' death. He didn't know how many times he'd tried to imagine his life without his own parents since he'd first learned about Lizzie's loss. Even if he didn't talk to his mom every day, he always knew she was there for him whenever he needed her. There had been several times during the wedding planning when he'd noticed a deep sense of pain in Lizzie and knew she must be missing her parents more than ever.

"Thanks, Emma. I'll talk to you later." Lizzie ended the call and placed the phone on the table.

"Everything okay with them?" Ian returned to his seat with a plate of cookies and a glass of milk.

Lizzie nodded. "Neither one of them is sick. I worried I may have infected them at lunch."

"I bet they have super immune systems after all the things they've been exposed to on their mission trips."

"Emma's going to bring over some soup for dinner."

"You're looking better. Do you think you'll be okay on your own tonight?"

"I think the worst is past. At least I hope so."

"You're planning on going to work tomorrow, aren't you?"

"If I don't get sick during the night, yeah, I'll go in."

"Don't overdo it. I don't want to have to carry you down the aisle because you are overworked."

Lizzie giggled. "That would be something new, wouldn't it?"

"Let's not find out." Ian winked and popped a cookie into his mouth.

CHAPTER THIRTEEN

Afternoons were always the busiest time at the front desk. The check-in line was ten deep when Stephen stepped out of the front office and into the lobby. He stayed close to the wall, praying his Jello-like legs would hold him up. The stretch of lobby before him, with no wall to cling to, loomed as wide as a football field.

At the end of the line he noticed a well-dressed woman, shuffling her feet, unfolding then refolding a piece of paper, her impatience evident with every move she made. Without seeing her face he knew it was Elaine Henderson and he felt his already sick stomach tighten. He eased his way back along the wall to the office door and stepped inside.

The only other person in the office was a girl working the room assignment desk, blocking rooms for the remainder of the week. Stephen made his way back to his desk and sank into his chair, then opened his instant messenger program. Ben and Jessica both showed online so he typed a message to Ben, describing Ms. Henderson and advising that she was in line at this very moment.

Ben's reply came back in a matter of seconds. *Finishing up another check-in right now. I'll get to her in a minute.*

Stephen tapped on the edge of the keyboard, hoping Ben would write again when he had Elaine at the desk. Five minutes passed, then ten. He didn't hear any yelling coming from the desk area, which he took to be a good sign. Elaine hadn't been happy the first time Stephen had checked her in, believing only Lizzie could take care of her. Maybe she didn't realize Ben wasn't Stephen.

Fifteen minutes later and Ben pushed through the door from the desk area. "Whew, that was quite a rush we had. Only twenty more check-ins for the day, though."

"How did it go with Ms. Henderson?"

"Piece of cake." Ben grinned. "She called me Stephen a few times and I wasn't about to correct her."

Stephen looked at him. Ben was five feet, seven inches tall, with broad shoulders, muscular arms, and sandy brown hair. The only physical trait the two men shared were their brown eyes. Stephen shook his head. "Goes to show she isn't very observant, but I'm glad she didn't give you any trouble."

"Are you feeling better?"

"I don't see a steak dinner in my future, but a bowl of soup might be nice. I was heading to the cafeteria when I saw her in line. I ducked back in here as quickly as I could."

"You want me to walk down there with you? I could use a soda."

"Sure." Stephen got to his feet and wobbled to the door.

When he stumbled outside the office, catching himself on a chair, Ben asked if he should get him a wheelchair.

"No, just give me a minute. We're almost to the service corridor. I can lean on the wall there."

"I sure hope you don't get any of us sick," Ben said, taking a step away.

"Yeah, me too. Lizzie would kill me." Stephen took a few tentative steps, picking up his pace when his legs didn't give out.

In another minute, they passed through a pair of doors to the service corridor. Stephen leaned against the wall and caught his breath.

"You sure you don't want a wheelchair? It's going to take forever to get to the cafeteria at this rate.

"You go on. I'll be fine." He reached into his pocket and pulled out his wallet. He handed Ben a five-dollar bill. "Will you get me some soup and a water?"

"Sure." Ben took the money, holding it by one corner, and took off at a brisk clip.

Stephen moved one step at a time. When he came to the group manager's office, he glanced inside, but Melvin wasn't there. He considered stopping to see if there was anything on the man's desk indicating where he might be, but a wave of dizziness hit him. He pressed on and reached the cafeteria where he saw Ben was already at the cash register.

Stephen dropped into the booth closest to the door and waved when Ben looked in his direction. Ben carried over a tray with a bottle of water, cup of soda, and a bowl on it. He set the bowl and water in front of Stephen, handing him a spoon, some napkins and his change, before taking a seat himself.

"Thanks," Stephen said. He dipped his spoon into the soup then halted with it halfway to his mouth at the sound of arguing voices, growing louder by the second.

In horror, Stephen watched Chef Gustave chase Melvin out of the kitchen that served both the cafeteria and the main dining room. Melvin cast Stephen a terrified glance as he raced past the booth and out the door. Stephen hoped the chef hadn't seen him and would return to the kitchen, but Chef Gustave continued in his direction.

"When is that imbecile ever going to be replaced?" Chef Gustave barked when he reached Stephen's table.

"I don't know," Stephen said. "Lizzie has told the general manager he isn't doing well."

"Isn't doing well? He's a disaster. He doesn't know a soufflé from a quiche and can't carry on a conversation for five minutes without getting distracted. He isn't welcome in my kitchen anymore!" The chef banged the table with his fist then turned and stalked back to the kitchen.

"I haven't seen Chef that mad in a long time," Ben said.

Stephen slurped at his soup. "I don't blame him. Melvin is awful."

"Why don't you or Lizzie take the job?"

"Lizzie enjoys the event planning more than I do, but I think she worries about who will take her place if she offers to take on the groups."

"You could take her place. They've already made you assistant manager; not that big a leap to make you manager."

"Yeah." Stephen twirled his spoon in his soup, bringing carrots and noodles to the surface before letting them fall back into the broth.

"You don't want to be the manger?" Ben asked.

"I don't know. To be honest, I never thought I'd be at the hotel this long."

"What do you want then?"

"I'm not sure anymore." Stephen lifted the spoon to his mouth and focused on finishing his meal.

CHAPTER FOURTEEN

Traffic crawled along Interstate-4. Jeffrey turned the radio up, hoping the positive music would cool his temper. His exit had been within sight for the past fifteen minutes, but he'd only moved twenty feet. Several cars had blown past on the shoulder, cutting back into traffic right before the exit. It took all his restraint not to edge over onto the shoulder, blocking anyone else from doing the same. The radio DJ came on as "The Little Drummer Boy" faded out. "Now here's a favorite of mine by 4Him, 'A Strange Way to Save the World'."

Cars inched forward, and by the time the song had ended, Jeffrey was gliding down the exit. He navigated the side streets with ease, pulling into his driveway a few minutes later. The bungalow he rented was on the edge of Nancy and Jason Edgewood's property. They'd had it built as an in-law suite, but neither set of parents was ready to move in, so they rented it out. Jeffrey could smell burgers on a grill and caught sight of a plume of smoke coming from his landlord's back patio. He waved at Jason who motioned for Jeffrey to come up.

Jeffrey crossed the large yard, skirted the pool, and joined Jason by the grill. "Smells good."

"Nancy is out of town visiting her sister so I get to have red meat."

"Is that unusual?"

Jason waved his spatula in the air. "Nancy is on an environmental kick. Cows are bad for the environment so we shouldn't encourage cattle farmers. Most of the time we're on the same page when it comes to our causes, but I can't get onboard with this one."

Jeffrey grinned. "I don't know many men who'd give up meat, especially a good steak."

"I went out for a steak last night, on the way home from dropping her off at the airport. Burgers tonight and ribs tomorrow. You care to join me?"

Jeffrey looked at the grill where four large burgers were sizzling. "If you have enough."

Jason guffawed. "I figured you'd be home about now and put two patties on for you. How do you like yours done?"

"Medium, with a hint of pink."

"Sounds good. Hand me that plate." Jason pointed to a large platter on the patio table.

"What other plans do you have while Nancy is gone?" Jeffrey handed Jason the plate and stood back while he flipped the burgers one more time.

"Not much. I should take the opportunity to get her Christmas gifts, but I never seem to get around to that until a couple of days beforehand."

"I know what you mean. Last year I was out Christmas Eve, trying to get everything I needed. I don't think I saw a single woman shopping."

"They're too busy at home cooking and wrapping. There are a couple of guys I see every year. We go to the same jewelry store around three o'clock Christmas Eve. The first couple of times it was a funny coincidence, but I think we've tacitly agreed to meet there each year now."

"You're kidding."

"No, sir. I don't know their names, but they're always there. I think they'd miss me if I did my shopping early. How about you? Any big plans this week?"

"I may check out a new group at church Wednesday night."

Jason piled the burgers onto the plate and turned the grill off. "I noticed you've been staying in more. Everything all right?"

The men moved to the table and pulled open buns. Jeffrey poured ketchup on one side and spread mayonnaise on the other, then added a slice of tomato, pickles, and finally his burger. A bowl of barbecue potato chips sat in the middle of the table. Jeffrey grabbed a couple handfuls and put them on his plate.

"I guess I'm still transitioning into a lifestyle that is more God-centered and less self-centered."

Jason bit into his burger, chewing for several minutes before swallowing and dabbing a spot of ketchup at the edge of his mouth. "Have you thought about getting involved in any charity work?"

"I can't say that I have. Did you have something particular in mind?"

"No, but it's a good way to meet people, make some new friends."

Jeffrey grimaced. "Everyone seems concerned about me finding friends."

"What you do is your business, but if you decide you want to get involved, let me know and I'll see what I can do to introduce you to the right people."

"I know you and Nancy do a lot of good things with your groups. I'll think about it."

Jason nodded. "So, are you free for dinner tomorrow night? How do you like your ribs?"

"Smothered in barbecue sauce and falling off the bone."

"I can manage that. Come on up when you get home."

CHAPTER FIFTEEN

Loud music jarred Lizzie from a deep sleep. She rolled over and slapped the snooze button. She'd made it through the night without any more sickness, but she wasn't ready to get out of bed just yet. Ten minutes later, the music blared again.

She groaned and pulled herself into a sitting position before turning off the alarm and heading for the shower. She turned the water on and stood in front of the mirror, waiting for the water to warm up.

She hadn't looked in the mirror since she'd fallen ill and was appalled by her appearance. Her face was like chalk and her eyes seemed supernaturally blue in an unsettling way. She ran her fingers through her hair, disgusted with the knots her curls had created. Since Ian had proposed in April she'd been growing it long for the wedding. He must love her if he wanted to marry her after seeing her this way.

Forty-five minutes later, she picked up a travel mug of coffee, grabbed her purse and stumbled out the front door. Her legs still felt shaky and it took a moment to catch her breath when she got in her car.

She reveled in her short commute to work and was crossing the hotel lobby ten minutes later. She waved at the front desk agents as she passed, hoping she didn't look as weak as she felt. The back office was quiet when she entered, but a light shone from the front office manager's doorway. She stopped and looked inside.

"Hi, Jonathan," she said.

Jonathan, a short man in his mid-forties with sparse black hair and dull green eyes, looked up. "Are you feeling better?"

"Good enough."

"Glad to hear it."

"Did I miss anything yesterday?"

"Not that I know of."

"Good." Lizzie let her purse slide off her shoulder and held the strap in her hand. "I'll be in my office if you need me."

Jonathan nodded and turned back to the paper he'd been reading.

The door from the lobby opened and Lizzie turned to see Ben enter. He stopped when he saw her, a smile brightening his face.

"It's good to see you." He moved closer. "Let me take your bag for you."

Before she could stop him, Ben had taken her purse and tucked her arm into his, escorting her to her desk.

"What's going on, Ben?"

He set her purse on the desk and released her arm. "Can't I be happy to see you?"

"I was only out one day. You weren't this happy to see me after I'd been gone for almost a week."

"Let's say I have a new appreciation for all you do here."

Lizzie narrowed her eyes and gave Ben what she hoped was an intimidating stare. "What does that mean? Where's Stephen?"

"I think he's in the kitchen talking with Chef. Melvin peeved Chef yesterday...big time."

Lizzie groaned and sank into her chair. "I was hoping Melvin might be able to hang in a couple more months, but if he keeps upsetting Chef..." Her voice trailed off as she considered the possibility that Chef Gustave would leave the hotel himself.

"Why don't you tell Mr. Kingsley you want to take over the group job and give this one to Stephen?"

"Don't think I haven't considered it." Lizzie rubbed her forehead. "I don't want Stephen to feel like he has to stay here, though."

"What else is he going to do?"

"He has options." Lizzie didn't know if Stephen had told anyone else about the offer he'd received several months before to move into human resources. Lizzie stood up. "I should go talk to Chef."

"All right. I'll handle things here; we have a light day."

"Thanks, Ben." Lizzie placed a hand on his shoulder as she passed him. "I'll be back soon."

She made her way down the service corridor and into the kitchen. The cooks were busy wrapping up breakfast service, the dishwashers a hive of activity as they were emptied and refilled from trays that came came in from the dining room. The noises were so familiar that she no longer noticed them as she moved toward Chef Gustave's office. She could see the chef at his desk, Stephen seated across from him. She stopped a few feet from the door and stepped to the side, so Chef wouldn't see her if he looked into the kitchen.

"I don't know what we'll do," Stephen was saying, "but I promise we'll do something about Melvin this week."

"You or Lizzie should take that job. I don't know why it hasn't been offered to either of you," Chef said.

"I don't mind helping out now and then, but event planning isn't my thing. I may be able to convince Lizzie to take it on if I agree to take her job."

"So why not do that?"

"It's complicated."

"Sounds easy to me. Lizzie is good with groups, you've gotten good with people. *Voilà*, perfect!"

Lizzie entered the office and placed a hand on the back of Stephen's chair. "No, it's not perfect. Stephen might want to do something else."

"Lizzie!" Stephen said as he jumped up and turned to her, his eyebrows raised in surprise.

"You look pale," she said. "Are you okay?"

"A little tired. How are you?"

"Better. Sorry about yesterday."

"What else might Stephen want to do?" Chef cut in. "You've been training him to be you."

Lizzie couldn't help but smile. Chef Gustave wasn't one to mince his words. "He finished his training months ago," she told him, "and he's become an excellent concierge, but he may have found something he's even better at."

"Such as?"

"That's for him to decide." Lizzie glanced at Stephen and saw how uncomfortable he was. "For now, we have to figure out a way to work with Melvin. Even if I take on the job full-time, I have a wedding coming up. I couldn't start until after that."

Chef gave a sullen nod. "Yes, your wedding is more important. If you promise Melvin will be gone when you return, I will find a way to work with him."

CHAPTER SIXTEEN

The service corridor was quiet when Lizzie and Stephen left the kitchen. Lizzie stayed close to the wall, still feeling weak. She wasn't sure if she would be able to make it through the whole day. Out of the corner of her eye, she noticed Stephen was walking equally close to the opposite wall.

"You're sick, aren't you?" she said.

"Why do you say that?"

Lizzie stopped and leaned against the wall. "You're pale and you're hugging that wall as much as I am."

"I didn't want to block the way in case a cart needed to be pushed through."

"Really? Then walk ahead of me. Go on, down the middle of the hall."

Stephen hesitated, then took several steps forward.

"Stop," Lizzie called and moved to catch up. "That doesn't prove anything, but I appreciate your bravery. Were you sick yesterday, too?"

"Maybe a little bit."

Lizzie linked her arm through his and they walked on again. "If you were anywhere near as sick as I was, then I am sorry. You should go home and rest."

"What about you?"

"I rested yesterday. If I stay at my desk the rest of the day, I'm sure I'll be fine."

They reached the hotel lobby and passed through the open space, finding a line of guests waiting at the front desk. Lizzie saw Ben and Jessica both manning it along with two front desk agents.

"I should get out there to help," Stephen said.

"Absolutely not." Lizzie squeezed his arm. "You're going home. Ben and Jessica can handle things."

Stephen reached for the office door and waited for Lizzie to pass through. She went straight to his desk and picked up his messenger bag.

"I don't need to go home," he insisted.

"Yes, you do. Get some sleep and be sure to drink lots of fluids. If you don't feel better tomorrow, stay home."

Stephen nodded and accepted his bag. Lizzie wondered if she'd done the right thing until a wave of dizziness made her grasp the chair at Stephen's desk. If she was still this off balance after a day of rest, he must be in even worse shape. When she regained her balance she made her way into her office and booted up her computer. If she could just make it until noon, she could consider leaving early.

CHAPTER SEVENTEEN

More cars filled the church parking lot than Jeffrey had expected for a Wednesday night. He found an empty space, then hurried across the asphalt toward the large building he knew hosted Sunday school classes. He pulled open the glass door and stepped inside, hoping there would be directions to the men's Bible study group.

The enticing scent of spaghetti drifted down the hall and he followed it until he reached a spacious room filled with round tables, almost every seat occupied.

"Can I help you?" A young lady in a pair of jeans and a red blouse approached Jeffrey.

Her face was open and kind and vaguely familiar, but Jeffrey's tension increased as she stepped closer. I'm not ready for this, he thought, starting to edge back from the doorway.

She studied him. "You're friends with Michelle, right?"

He stopped and looked at the woman. Her brown hair fell around her shoulders, her eyes large. The more he stared the more certain he was he'd met her before, but couldn't remember where.

"Wendy; we met at Will's Pub last year."

"Right, you work with Michelle. You're the one she thought would enjoy the show that night. Wow, how've you been?"

"I can't complain. Aside from Amanda's death, it's been a quiet year."

"Yeah, sorry about that."

"Not your fault," she said with a shrug. "Come on in, have some dinner."

"I already ate." Jeffrey stepped back into the hall.

"Are you here for Bible study then?" She checked her watch. "That starts in fifteen minutes. There are a couple of different groups. Which one are you looking for?"

Jeffrey's shoulders slumped. "I'm not sure. I read online about a men's Bible study here."

Wendy smiled and nodded. "Sure, why don't I take you to the room they meet in? A few of the guys are probably already there. Wait here a second."

Jeffrey watched as she jogged back to a table, spoke with one of the ladies seated there, then collected her purse and Bible. She rejoined him and motioned that he follow her.

"Have you talked to Michelle lately?" she asked.

Jeffrey shook his head.

"You should call her. She needs to get out more."

"People keep telling me I need to get out more," Jeffrey replied stiffly. "Why is solitude such a bad thing?"

Wendy stopped and turned to face him. "In small doses it's a great thing, gives us time to recharge, reconnect with God, evaluate where we are, but when we aren't getting out and socializing we get tied up in ourselves. That rarely leads to good things."

Jeffrey felt his fingers clenching into fists. What right did this stranger have to criticize him? Just because he was spending a lot time alone didn't mean he'd stopped caring about other people. It just happened that the people he cared about had lives of their own and he couldn't always be the third wheel.

He felt a gentle touch on his arm and looked down to see Wendy's hand retreating.

"I'm not criticizing," she said as her hand dropped to her side. "I understand how hard it is to transition from a life of serving self to a life of serving God.

"I grew up in church, but in college I drifted away and only after Amanda's death did I think about returning to church. If it hadn't been for one of the ladies I met in worship service one week, I may not be here today. She's mentored me and helped me make friends. Let me do that for you."

Jeffrey relaxed his fists, his fingers twitching as the fight-or-flight adrenaline drained away, leaving a pit in his stomach. Wendy moved away and he followed.

They climbed a flight of stairs and walked down a hallway. Jeffrey could hear laughter and banging noises. They approached a doorway and he slowed, allowing Wendy to get several feet ahead. This was his last chance to back out. At the door Wendy stopped and looked his way. Jeffrey took a deep breath and followed her inside.

He scanned the room. Several game tables filled one end and the other was set up with folding chairs. A few men were already seated, deep in conversation.

Wendy approached a squat man with thinning black hair. He pulled her into a bear hug when she tapped him on the shoulder. Jeffrey watched as they exchanged words, then the man came over with Wendy.

"Chad, this is Jeffrey. He's new to the group."

"Nice to meet you, Jeffrey." Chad held out his hand and Jeffrey shook it. "Come on in and I'll introduce you to everyone."

"I'll see you around." Wendy winked then disappeared down the hall.

CHAPTER EIGHTEEN

Chad led Jeffrey toward the rows of chairs, then gave a loud whistle that brought an instant hush to the people around the game tables. The men made their way to the chairs and took their seats.

"Everyone, I'd like you to meet Jeffrey," Chad said.

Jeffrey stuffed his hands in his pockets and looked around the room. He'd never been shy in a group before, but now he felt naked and vulnerable.

"Let's all take a seat and we'll get started," Chad said.

To Jeffrey's dismay his foot somehow became tangled in the feet of the closest chair, making a terrible clanging noise as he tried to step away. He could feel every pair of eyes on him. He weighed the options of bolting from the room right now, or waiting and making a more subdued escape later, maybe during the opening prayer. He opted for the latter and took a seat in a chair at the end of a row.

"It's good to see you all tonight," Chad said. "We're starting a new study on the apostle Paul and how the principles he taught the original church remain relevant today. Juan, will you open us in prayer?"

Jeffrey watched as all the men bowed their heads and closed their eyes. He prepared himself to move as soon as Juan started speaking.

"Dear Lord, thank you for the opportunity to gather together tonight to learn how to be better men."

Jeffrey lifted his bottom off the cold metal chair and straightened his legs, his movements so slow he could have been in a stop action film running a frame at a time.

"Thank you for bringing Jeffrey into our group, Lord. You know his needs and I have faith you will show us how to minister to him."

Jeffrey froze at the mention of his name. He heard several of the men closest to him whisper "Yes, Lord" and saw them nod their heads. These guys didn't even know him, so why were they praying for him?

"I pray you will open our hearts and our minds to the lesson you have for us tonight. In your precious name we pray, Amen."

Jeffrey settled back into his seat as the men around him echoed the "Amen" and raised their heads.

"Thank you, Juan." Chad stood at the front of the room and opened his Bible. "Most of us know the story of Paul. He was a highly esteemed leader of the Jewish people, and he was certain, beyond a shadow of a doubt, that those who had taken to following Jesus, and the disciples He left behind to spread His gospel, were enemies of the Jews. They were blasphemers and deserved punishment, even death. I don't know how much blood he had on his hands before he made his trip to Damascus, yet God chose to use Paul, and changed his heart forever."

Chad paused and looked around the room. Jeffrey met his gaze for a moment then looked away. He'd heard about Paul in church a few times and he seemed to remember Lizzie mentioning him at some point as well. As Jeffrey listened to Chad tell them how Paul had been changed from one who persecuted the new Christians to one who became a dominant leader of the Christian faith, he was struck by how instantaneous that change seemed to have taken place.

Jeffrey tried to reconcile this with the struggles he himself had faced, longing to return to his old life. Had it been easier for Paul because he was already a religious man?

Chad continued teaching but Jeffrey's mind was stuck on Paul's conversion experience. After the closing prayer, he began to stand when the man sitting on his left spoke to him.

"What do you think of our group?"

"Interesting stuff," Jeffrey mumbled.

"I'm Paul, by the way." The man held out his hand.

"You're joking, right?"

The man looked puzzled then chuckled. "You mean because of the lesson? No, that's really my name."

Jeffrey shook his hand, still not sure what to think. "Nice to meet you, Paul."

"I saw you come in with Wendy. Are you two friends?"

"We have a mutual friend."

"She seems like a nice girl."

"Yeah, I guess so." Jeffrey stood up and Paul did too.

"You want to get a cup of coffee?" Paul asked.

Jeffrey stepped out of the row of chairs and turned toward the door. "Why?"

Paul looked surprised. "Just trying to be friendly. You looked like you had a lot on your mind, but I didn't figure you'd want to talk with so many people around. I was the new guy once, too, but if I was wrong then I apologize."

That doesn't mean you have to close yourself off from other relationships. Lizzie's words echoed in Jeffrey's mind. I don't think this is the type of relationship she was referring to, he thought.

"I do have a lot on my mind," Jeffrey said. "I don't know if I'm ready to discuss it, though."

"Fair enough. We can still get some coffee and get to know each other. I have a feeling we have a lot in common."

Jeffrey eyed the man, noticing that Paul wore an Atlanta Braves polo and jeans, and realized he was wearing the same team's polo himself. At least they had baseball in common. What could a cup of coffee hurt?

CHAPTER NINETEEN

Jeffrey was surprised to find the usually crowded Starbucks deserted when he entered. The barista asked if he'd like to try a Gingerbread latte, but he declined, ordering a grande Cafe Americano instead. The front door opened while the barista was preparing his drink and Paul entered.

"Can I get a tall Caramel Macchiato, please?" Paul paid for his drink before stepping to the end of the counter where Jeffrey stood. "What do you think the chances are of the Braves winning the Series next year?"

Jeffrey shrugged and accepted his coffee from the barista. "They had a good run this year. If they can hold it together, maybe they can make it all the way."

"Have you been to any of the spring training games out at Disney?" Paul accepted his cup and the two men moved to a pair of leather chairs in the back corner of the cafe.

"It's been a while. This project I'm working on has kept me busy the past three years."

"What do you do?"

"I'm a project manager for Hollisbrook Construction. I've been overseeing construction of The Plaza in downtown."

"I know the site. My girlfriend has been drooling over the condo concepts for months. Between the two of us, we couldn't begin to afford one of those places, but it doesn't hurt for her to dream."

"They *are* going to be pricy." Jeffrey sipped his coffee.

Paul settled back in his seat and lifted his coffee to his mouth, prolonging the silence between them. Jeffrey felt like he should say something, ask what Paul did or about his girlfriend, but he really didn't care. Why had he agreed to this?

"I've seen you in church services for several months. Why did you decide to join the Bible study tonight?"

Well, I guess the small talk is over, thought Jeffrey. He rested the coffee cup on his knee and stared at the floor. "I need to meet new people."

Paul gave a slight nod, but didn't respond. Jeffrey tapped the side of his cup, waiting for the other man to say something. Paul's face was serene, his grey eyes never wavering from Jeffrey.

"I became a Christian a year ago and had to stop hanging out with most of the guys I knew before," Jeffrey found himself saying. "My best friend is getting married in a couple of weeks and I told her I'd have a date, but I don't because I don't know any Christian women. Even my assistant accused me of isolating myself so I decided to come to Bible study tonight."

Paul smiled. "That wasn't so hard, was it?"

"You work for the CIA, don't you?" Jeffrey felt a bead of sweat on his temple.

Paul's laughter was warm and filled the entire room. "I didn't waterboard you, I just gave you time to speak."

"I think I would have preferred waterboarding. You're so calm, and your eyes; I feel like they can see right through me."

"I'll remember that for next time. Back to this date for the wedding. You aren't planning on taking another guy are you?"

Jeffrey was caught off guard, then chuckled. "No, I didn't come to church looking for a date, unless of course you know someone who wouldn't feel awkward going to a wedding with someone she doesn't know."

Paul scratched his head. "I might."

Jeffrey couldn't believe his luck, but then again, could he go to Lizzie's wedding with a complete stranger? There would be so many questions to answer.

"Let me think about it and get back to you. In the meantime, tell me more about yourself. How did you come to Christ?"

Michelle was the only person Jeffrey had told the whole story. He was sure Paul would get up and walk out when he heard about Jeffrey's wild past. Michelle had been different. She'd known him before his transformation. It had taken her months, though, to believe he'd truly changed.

"You know how it is; rebellious youth, trouble with the parents, running with a rowdy crowd. One night it wasn't enough. My life was empty and I realized I wanted the peace and strength I saw in my friend Lizzie. I showed up on her doorstep in the middle of the night and she took me through the steps of accepting God as my savior."

"How hard has it been to stay on your new path?"

Jeffrey sighed. "Some days are easier than others. I cut out the people I used to see socially. My relationship with my parents is better, but still rocky at times. I spend a lot more time at home."

"It's good you came tonight. I think this new Bible study will be helpful."

"It sounds like Saint Paul had it all together the moment he became a believer. I wish my transformation had been so easy and complete."

Paul leaned forward and looked Jeffrey in the eye. "You think his transformation was easy? He lived in the time of Jesus. If he didn't see Jesus preach or witness any of the miracles himself, then he certainly knew people who had. Still, he was filled with anger and hatred for Jesus and those who followed Him. It took being blinded in the desert, hearing God speak to him directly, and waiting three days for another man to remove from his eyes the scales God had used to blind him, for Paul to become a believer. After that, yes, his transformation was complete, but I wouldn't say it was easy."

CHAPTER TWENTY

Exhaust fumes overwhelmed Michelle when she stepped out of the elevator into the parking garage. She'd spent most of the day on the phone with clients looking to maximize their investments in a volatile market. Her head hurt from staring at the computer screen without a break, and the fumes seemed to increase the pain tenfold.

She ducked into her car and cranked the engine. Her cell phone chirped with a new text message and she was surprised to see Jeffrey's name on the phone's display.

Know it's last min but wondered if u wanted a bite tonight? Leaving site now.

She thumbed in a response, agreeing to meet him at Houlihan's in ten minutes, and received a smiley face in return a few seconds later. Traffic was light for a Friday afternoon, allowing her to make it to the restaurant in record time. She tried to fluff her hair with a couple of passes of her hairbrush, freshened up her lipstick then slipped out of the car. Jeffrey was waiting by the front door. When she met his gaze and he smiled, her stomach fluttered. What was that, she wondered. I hope I'm not getting sick.

"Thanks for meeting me," he said as he opened the door for her.

"I had planned to go out with Wendy tonight, but she left early with a migraine."

"I'm sorry to hear that. I hope she feels better soon. Did the two of you have any particular plans? We could do that instead, if you prefer."

"We were going to get dinner and catch a movie. It's the first weekend I haven't had a show in over a month, so we were just going to chill out."

The hostess led them to a table and handed them menus. "Your server will be with you in a few minutes."

"Did you have a nice Thanksgiving?" Jeffrey asked.

"I went to see my parents. You?"

"My parents are in Barbados, but Lizzie had several friends over." Jeffrey chuckled. "One day I will remember her food is never free."

Michelle tensed at the mention of Lizzie's name. "What do you mean?"

"After dinner, she had a project for us to do in the backyard. I have to admit, though, she has a good eye for design."

"Her wedding's soon, isn't it?"

"Two weeks from tomorrow."

Michelle noticed his grimace. "What's wrong?""

"It's nothing."

A server arrived and they gave him their orders.

Michelle unwrapped the napkin holding her silverware and smoothed it on the table. "I thought you were happy they are getting married."

"I am. Ian is good for Lizzie."

"So what's bothering you?"

Jeffrey reached for the ketchup bottle at the edge of the table and flipped the lid up and down. Michelle placed her hand on his, then eased the bottle away from him. Jeffrey looked up and met her gaze. There was that strange flutter again.

Jeffrey slumped in his seat. "I don't have a date. I don't know why I told her I would. It's not like I even know many women."

Michelle leaned back and studied him. She'd accepted his complete change of lifestyle months ago, but it still surprised her to hear he was at a loss to find a date.

"It's no big deal. I'll call her this weekend so she can make whatever last minute adjustments are needed. I'm sure there will be someone else there alone, too." Jeffrey leaned forward and his face brightened. "The stuffed chicken breast you ordered sounds good. I always get a burger or steak when I come here. Maybe next time I'll try the chicken."

"I love anything with cream cheese," Michelle grinned. As if on cue, the server returned with their plates.

CHAPTER TWENTY-ONE

A car alarm outside the apartment window woke Michelle from a deep sleep. She groaned and pulled a pillow over her head, but the noise didn't stop. Kicking off the covers, she stretched and sat up. The clock on the bedside table read seven twenty-five.

"The one day I can sleep in and some idiot robs me of that." She stood and shuffled into the living room where there was a window overlooking the parking lot. Her car was at the edge of her field of vision, but its lights weren't flashing. All looked quiet in this section of the lot.

She moved to the front door, but before she could open it, the alarm fell silent. She rubbed her eyes and considered returning to bed, but knew she'd never get back to sleep.

"What a way to start the day," she grumbled as she poured water into the coffee pot. While she waited for it to brew, she pulled her favorite coffee cup from the cabinet. It bore a cartoon of a jazz trio with the words "Keep it Smooth" printed in purple.

When the coffee was ready, she filled the cup, adding a dash of sugar and a sprinkling of cinnamon, then moved to the couch and reached for the television remote. The news was talking about the upcoming election in Iraq, raising hopes that a new parliament could pave the way for American troops to return home. She flipped to another channel, where a woman was trying on wedding dresses.

Michelle watched for several minutes, amused by the comments of the bride's friends each time she came out of the dressing room. One didn't have a single positive word. The dress was either too tight or too short, or too frilly. On the fifth dress, the bride lost it and started yelling at her friend. Michelle rolled her eyes and flipped the channel again.

A commercial for a carpet steamer, a show on the mating habits of African dwarf frogs, a sitcom that had been in syndication for twenty years, nothing caught her attention. She returned to the wedding show in time to see the dress the bride ended up choosing. The friend who'd been so critical was no longer in the dress shop, which made Michelle smile.

She found herself wondering what kind of dress Lizzie had chosen for her wedding. She imagined something with a high neck, long sleeves, and loose as a potato sack. She reached for her cell phone and texted her friend Matt.

You awake?

Her phone gave a staccato burst in response a few minutes later. *Barely. What's up?*

Michelle chose the speed dial assigned to Matt and waited for him to answer.

"Why are you up so early?" His voice was still thick with sleep.

"Car alarm woke me. You?"

"I'm supposed to be going for a jog. I don't see that happening."

"When did you start running?"

"I haven't, but there is this cute girl I met at Starbucks. She mentioned she runs every Saturday. I was going to try to accidentally run into her."

Michelle laughed. "Why didn't you just ask her out at Starbucks?"

"I was embarrassed. This girl is fit. I don't think there is an ounce of body fat on her."

"You aren't a lump of lard yourself."

"I haven't been to the gym in months and I've put on a few pounds. All these late nights with the band are catching up with me."

"I know what you mean." Michelle yawned.

"So, what's up with you?"

"I saw Jeffrey last night."

"Yeah, and?"

"He mentioned he didn't have a date for Lizzie's wedding, but he didn't ask me to go with him."

"Why would he? It's not like the two of you are dating."

"Thank you. I keep telling Wendy we aren't dating, but she doesn't believe me."

"Are you bothered he didn't ask you to the wedding?"

"I wasn't, but now, I don't know. Why wouldn't he? He's been trying to get me to meet Lizzie for more than a year."

"I wouldn't take any girl I wasn't serious about to a wedding. Even then, I'd have to make sure she knew we weren't the next couple heading down the aisle."

"You think Jeffrey was worried I'd interpret it the wrong way if he asked me to go?"

"Maybe, or maybe he's just not into you. Weddings are great places to meet chicks. The single ones are always depressed they're still alone and they eat up any attention they are given."

"Matt! You're awful." Michelle tried to picture her friend hitting on girls at a wedding.

"I'm just telling you what I've seen. Maybe you and I should find a wedding to crash this weekend, see if we can meet any new people."

"What about your Starbucks girl?"

"I'll see her when I see her. I'm not looking for anything serious, just a little fun."

Michelle shook her head. "I've never seen this side of you."

"I'm not getting any younger. Sooner or later I'll have to grow up, but until then..."

"It's always great to get the uncensored male view on things from you."

"Any time. What are your plans today?"

"I don't know. I need to get groceries, but I'm not up for that yet. What are you doing, since you gave up running?"

"I think I'll go to the gym. Maybe I will find a cute girl to chat up."

"You're impossible."

"That's why you love me, isn't it?"

"I guess. Have a good time."

"See you tonight."

Michelle hung up and returned to the kitchen to refill her coffee cup.

CHAPTER TWENTY-TWO

An electronic bell sounded when Lizzie and Stephanie entered the bridal boutique. The shop was light and airy, several dozen dress styles on display around the perimeter of the main room. A sales clerk in a pale grey suit emerged from the back and greeted them with a bright smile.

"Ms. Reynolds, Ms. Jordanopolous, it's good to see you again. Only a couple more weeks until the big day." The clerk paused and frowned. "You look like you've lost weight, Ms. Reynolds."

"I had the flu," Lizzie said. "I couldn't have lost more than a pound or two, though."

The clerk gave a sympathetic nod. "I had it a few weeks ago. I hope you are feeling better."

"Much," Lizzie assured her.

"Then let's get to the dresses. Is Ms. Pierce coming as well?"

"She should be here any minute."

"You go on back. I can wait for Mona," Stephanie offered.

Lizzie followed the clerk through a pair of thick curtains. Instead of the typical fluorescent lights, several chandeliers cast a warm yellow glow on the thick ivory carpet and chocolate suede sofas. Even after a dozen visits she still felt like she was entering the dressing room of a princess. Her pulse quickened at the sight of her dress, waiting for her on the front of a changing room door. Cap sleeves led down to a fitted bodice with a slight flare below the hips. Lace covered the dress, but it wasn't frilly. A hand-beaded Grosgrain sash added a touch of elegance.

"Would you like me to help you?" the clerk asked.

"Here we are," Stephanie said, pushing through the curtains and followed by Mona, her cheeks flushed.

"Sorry I'm late. There was a wreck that had traffic tied up for miles. I detoured around it as soon as I came to a side street."

"Sit down and catch your breath. I'll get you a glass of water," the clerk said.

Mona sank onto one of the sofas and dropped her purse on the floor. "I can't believe it's almost Christmas and still eighty degrees outside."

Lizzie laughed. "After living here for fifteen years, you should be used to this by now."

"You're right, but my brain doesn't seem capable of connecting Christmas with hot weather."

"Here you are." The clerk returned with a glass of water. Mona accepted it and swallowed it in one long gulp.

"Thank you." Mona stood and moved toward the door where Lizzie's gown hung. "I just love this dress. The ivory is a perfect complement for your skin tone."

Lizzie had been relieved when no one had questioned why she hadn't chosen a pure white dress. Even though she knew she'd been washed clean of her past sins, she hadn't felt she could wear white. She knew most people thought a woman saving herself until marriage was an archaic idea, one she'd certainly screwed up, but she and Ian had made a commitment to each other that she was proud of.

Stephanie gathered Lizzie's long hair in her hands and held it up. "Have you decided how you are going to wear your hair?"

"Not yet. I've looked at so many different pictures I feel overwhelmed."

"You're going to have a headband similar to the sash, right? I think you should curl it and leave it down."

"You don't think I should pull it up in a bun or some kind of twist?"

"I agree with Stephanie," Mona said. "Even though your natural curls are weighed down by the extra length, after a few minutes on some rollers, your hair would be gorgeous."

"I still have a couple of days to think about it. Let's try on these dresses and get some lunch."

"Thank you for not making us wear something hideous." Stephanie smiled as she reached for her own dress. It was dove grey with a

Christmas plaid sash in red, green, and black. The full-length gown had a high neck and cap sleeves.

"It's ridiculously hard to find bridesmaid dresses that aren't awkward," Lizzie said as she stepped into her dressing room and shut the door. "Right after college, I was in three weddings and all the dresses were terrible. I donated them to a local theater to use in their wardrobe. If nothing else, the seamstress could take them apart and use the material for some kind of costume."

"That's a great idea." Mona's voice was muffled by the thin wall between them.

Lizzie stepped into her gown, settling the sleeves on her shoulders and struggling with the zipper as far as she could. She pushed open her door and the sales clerk moved to help. With the zipper done and the sash tied, she could tell the dress was looser than the last time she'd tried it on.

"I think you lost more than a pound while you were sick," the clerk said as she walked around Lizzie with a critical eye.

"I'm sure I'll gain it back between now and the wedding."

"Maybe." The clerk led Lizzie to a small dais in the middle of the room and helped her step onto it.

Lizzie saw her reflection in the mirror and felt her stomach tighten. She glanced toward a pair of empty chairs and felt tears stinging her eyes. I wish you were here, mom, she thought. Can you see me now?

"Oh, Lizzie," Stephanie breathed.

Lizzie turned to see her friend emerging from her own dressing room, the dove grey dress making the brown of her hair and eyes pop.

"Every time I see you in that dress it's more amazing than before," Stephanie said. "You're going to be the perfect bride."

"You aren't looking so bad yourself." Lizzie smiled at her friend, thankful for the distraction.

"I think something's wrong with my dress," Mona said, coming out of her dressing room, her dress puddling at her feet.

The clerk rushed to Mona's side. "Oh dear, the seamstress must have let out the hem instead of taking it up. Come, we'll get you pinned up and send it back today."

She led Mona to another dais, where the clerk started tucking and pinning until the dress was similar in length to Stephanie's. When the clerk was satisfied, the girls changed back into their own clothes.

"Ms. Reynolds, I think you should come back next week to make sure everything is all right. We have someone who can take care of a minor tuck if needed."

"I will have to check my schedule and call you for an appointment."

"That's fine. I want you to look perfect on your big day."

CHAPTER TWENTY-THREE

Lizzie fished a pair of sunglasses from the depths of her purse as she followed Stephanie and Mona out of the bridal shop. Christmas shoppers crowded the sidewalk, making it difficult for the women to stay together. Stephanie turned down a small alley, leaving the crowds behind. Lizzie moved beside her two friends and linked arms with them.

"Thank you both for agreeing to do this for me. I know we don't get together often outside of the Concierge Club dinners. When I started planning the wedding I realized how much I've let work take over my life."

"I'm honored you thought of me," Mona said.

"Me too. I thought you'd have Emma as your matron-of-honor." Stephanie held open a door and then followed the others inside.

Lizzie smiled at the hostess, who led them to a table and handed out menus. "I thought about it," Lizzie said when the hostess had left, "but she's as close to a mother as I have." Her voice caught in her throat.

Stephanie reached across the table and clasped Lizzie's hand. "You're always so strong I forget how hard it must be planning all this without your parents."

"Emma and Ron have been great, I know I'm lucky to have them, but sometimes..." Lizzie shrugged.

"I'm sure they are looking down from heaven and smiling on you," Mona said.

Lizzie nodded. "I believe that, and I know they would have loved Ian."

"Who doesn't? The guy's perfect." Stephanie sighed.

Mona giggled. "You're sure he doesn't have a brother?"

"Not that he's aware of. Don't worry your time will come, both of you."

A server delivered a basket of bread and took their orders. Stephanie reached for a piece of bread and tore off a corner. "Do you know if Stephen is bringing a date to the wedding?"

Lizzie suppressed a smile. "He's not. There are a few guys who will be there alone. I could introduce you to them."

"You're going to be too busy to introduce us to single guys," Mona said. "Just tell me what tables they're seated at and we can find them ourselves."

Lizzie laughed, relieved the sadness that had clutched her heart in the bridal shop was now fading away. She knew her parents would want her to enjoy every minute of this special time.

"When did you become so brazen?" Stephanie asked.

Mona blushed. "It sounded like a practical idea in my mind, but completely out of character when I said it."

"I remember the first day I met you," Lizzie said then turned to Stephanie. "I was working front desk at a Disney resort and noticed Mona loitering around the lobby a good twenty minutes before she came to the desk. I asked her how I could help and she asked what kind of shoes I was wearing.

"I thought that was strange but I told her, and even took one off to show her. That's when she told me she was going to start working with us the following week. We were on the same shift the day she started and her shoes were almost identical to mine."

All three women were laughing when the server returned with their food. The strange look he gave them made Lizzie laugh even harder. Why hadn't she done this more often, she wondered.

"I remember the first Concierge Club dinner Mona came to." Stephanie looked at Mona. "You were so quiet, I couldn't believe you were a concierge."

"Yeah, new settings are tough for me, but once I know the lay of the land I'm more comfortable."

"Well, you've been to Avalon Grove with me a couple of times to see different decorating schemes. Do you think you know the lay of the land well enough to approach a table of single guys?" Lizzie grinned.

"Maybe we could go by once more and they could show me where that particular table will be. I want to feel really comfortable." Mona giggled.

"I can arrange that. Stephanie, you want to come too?"

"Why not? I'm all about comfort."

Lizzie reached for her purse, found her phone, and punched in a number from memory.

"Now, after we finish eating, I think we should get some pedicures, and do a little shopping before heading over to Avalon Grove. I have a couple of Christmas gifts I still need to pick out."

CHAPTER TWENTY-FOUR

Ian drummed his fingers on the steering wheel, waiting for the car ahead of him to move forward. He'd hoped to be able to meet his parents in baggage claim, but their flight had landed ten minutes earlier. Even with the time it would take to get from the gate to baggage claim, and the subsequent delay of their bags arriving, he'd be lucky if he didn't leave them waiting on the curb. He crept forward, allowing his thoughts to drift. He was worried about Lizzie.

She was a master at hiding her feelings, but he could tell there was something bothering her. At dinner the previous night, they'd been discussing plans for the weekend, and his parents coming to town. As he'd talked about how excited his parents were about the wedding, she'd grown quiet. They'd continued talking, but there had been a look in her eyes that told him she wasn't engaged.

When he finally reached the airport, he did indeed find his parents waiting on the curb. His mother's face brightened with a wide smile as he pulled up beside them and stepped out of the car.

"It's so good to see you." Cassandra Cavanaugh pulled him into her arms.

"I hope you didn't have to wait too long. Traffic was backed up through the toll plaza." Ian reached for his mother's suitcase.

"Not long at all," Colin Cavanaugh said, lifting his own bag into the trunk of the car.

"Is Lizzie working?"

Ian grinned. "No, she let me borrow her car while she and her bridesmaids have their last dress fittings."

"Is there anything I can help her with? The last couple of weeks before a wedding can be hectic," Cassandra said as she ducked into the backseat as and her husband and son took their positions up front.

"I'm not sure. It sounds like everything is in place." Ian glanced into the rearview mirror and caught his mother's gaze. "I think she's missing her parents more than usual."

"That's understandable," Colin said.

Ian saw an opening in the traffic and pulled away from the curb. Several minutes later, he merged onto the highway.

"You don't think she'll mind that we came in so early, do you?" Concern was evident in Cassandra's tone, warming Ian's heart. He was grateful for the love his parents already felt for Lizzie.

He shrugged. "I don't think she minds, but it might be hard for her. Ron and Emma are wonderful, but..."

"No relationship can ever replace that of parent and child," Cassandra said.

Ian slowed for an exit ramp. "I wish I could take away her pain."

Colin nodded. "You know only God can do that."

"I know. I just feel so helpless sometimes. Maybe it would help if she talked about them more."

"She's dealt with her grief on her own for a long time. She'll talk when she's good and ready." Cassandra leaned forward and squeezed his shoulder.

Ian pulled into the Hotel Lago parking lot and helped his parents with their luggage. A bellman in a pair of dark pants and an ocean-blue polo shirt approached them with a wheeled cart.

"Good afternoon, Mr. and Mrs. Cavanaugh. Let me help you with those." Before Ian could protest, the bellman had freed Ian and Colin of the bags and placed them on his cart. "I'll take these up to the room while you check-in."

"Thank you." Ian gave a sheepish smile. "I guess Lizzie let everyone know you were arriving today."

The bellman preceded them into the lobby, and by the time they'd reached the front desk, Stephen was stepping through the office door.

"Mom, dad, this is Stephen: Lizzie's right hand man."

Stephen's face flushed. "Mr. and Mrs. Cavanaugh, welcome."

"Please, call us Cassie and Colin," Cassandra said. "It's nice to meet you."

"We have you in the Lake Trasimeno suite." Stephen hit several keys on the computer and a printer spit out two plastic key cards. "Your luggage should already be there. I'll meet you right around the corner and take you up to your room."

"That's not necessary," Colin said.

"I need to check on the concierge lounge anyway." Stephen nodded toward the hallway before slipping into the office.

Ian led his parents around the corner and met Stephen coming out the side door.

At the elevator, Stephen pressed a button and the doors slid open. He stepped inside and once everyone was onboard, pressed for the sixth floor. "Lizzie mentioned you are all going out to dinner tonight, but I can arrange for a snack if you are hungry now."

Colin glanced at Cassandra. "I'm fine, you?"

"I wouldn't mind a bottle of water. Flying always makes me feel dehydrated."

"We have Dasani and Evian in the lounge; do you have a preference?"

"Either one is fine, but I can get it, just show me the way."

The elevator opened and Stephen led them out of the sixth floor lobby into a spacious lounge. A four-foot tall Christmas tree was tucked into a corner, trimmed with ornaments in hues of blue and silver, and garlands were draped across each of the large windows. Through a set of French doors, Lake Eola glistened with the reflection of the late afternoon sun.

"What a view," Cassandra sighed.

"The lounge has light breakfast from seven to nine each morning, afternoon snacks from one to three, cocktails from five to six and desserts from seven to nine. There are sodas and bottled water in the fridge that you are welcome to anytime." Stephen opened the refrigerator and pulled out a bottle of water for Cassandra. "This way to your room."

They passed several doors before Stephen stopped, pulling one of the key cards from his pocket. He opened the double doors and stepped aside to allow the Cavanaughs to pass, and smiled when he heard Cassandra gasp.

The Lake Trasimeno suite was Stephen's favorite. Pale yellow walls exuded a Tuscan-like sun onto the polished wood floor. Two walnut Louis XIV armchairs covered in olive green velvet flanked the large window overlooking Lake Eola, a simple walnut desk between them. A comfortable empire-style settee covered in a Dijon mustard-colored fabric with whimsical brown curlicues faced a 32-inch flat screen television, one of the few modern touches in this antique-inspired room. An arched doorway led to the bedroom, which held a queen-sized bed under a cream duvet, accented with olive and gold throw pillows. A reading area furnished with a classic Erin chair, ottoman, and a pendant floor lamp added a cozy touch to offset the formal atmosphere.

Stephen watched with pride as Colin and Cassandra took it all in. Cassandra paused at the desk. "How did you know I love peonies?"

"Ian mentioned it to Lizzie a few months ago," Stephen said, "when she was looking at flowers for the wedding. She makes it a point to remember things like that."

"It's a lovely arrangement."

"Jackson – he's the owner of Fields of Bloom – does most of our flowers."

"He's doing the flowers for the wedding, too," Ian added.

"If you don't need anything else, I'll let you get settled." Stephen handed the key cards to Ian and pulled the door closed behind him.

"I told Lizzie we'd meet her at the restaurant at six thirty. There's plenty of time for you to take a nap if you'd like."

"We aren't that old and it was only a two hour flight," Cassandra protested.

"I wouldn't mind lying down for a little bit," Colin said.

"Why don't you guys unpack and I'll come by to pick you up at six?"

"That sounds fine," Colin agreed.

"I'm glad you're here." Ian gave his mother a hug and slipped out of the room.

CHAPTER TWENTY-FIVE

Jeffrey muted the television and reached for the ringing phone. "Hello?"

"Jeffrey, it's Paul, from church. Hope I'm not bothering you."

"Nah, I'm just chilling. What's up?"

"I've been thinking about your wedding date problem."

"Really?" Jeffrey ran a hand through his tousled hair. "It's no big deal. I'm going to call Lizzie tonight and tell her I'm not bringing anyone."

"Have you thought about asking Wendy? She's nice and you already kind of know her."

Jeffrey chuckled. "I know her through her friend Michelle. I can't ask Wendy if I'm not asking Michelle."

"Why aren't you asking Michelle, then?"

"It's complicated."

"How so?"

Jeffrey stood and paced around the living room. Did he want to get into this with a guy he scarcely knew? "It's a long story."

"I have time."

Jeffrey could picture Paul reclining on his couch, waiting for Jeffrey to spill his guts. "Your CIA mind tricks aren't going to work this time."

"I don't know what you mean."

Jeffrey could hear the smile in Paul's words and couldn't help grinning himself. He returned to the couch and sat down. "I don't want to give Michelle any mixed signals by asking her to the wedding. We've been hanging out for several months, but we're just friends."

"And you're worried she'll think you want more if you take her to the wedding?"

"Well, yeah."

"And you're not at all interested in her?"

Jeffrey rubbed his eyes. "That's where it gets complicated."

He leaned back on the couch, propping his feet up on the coffee table. When Paul didn't speak, Jeffrey knew the other man would remain silent until he laid out the whole story. After a five minute abbreviated version of his history with Michelle he concluded, "I thought I was getting through to her a few months ago, but I don't know, nothing seems to have changed."

"You're right, you shouldn't ask Michelle to the wedding, but that doesn't mean you can't ask Wendy."

"I don't know. I think I'd be more comfortable going alone."

"Does Michelle know you go to the same church as Wendy?"

"Only if Wendy's told her. I didn't even know myself until I saw her Wednesday."

"I wonder if ... never mind."

"What?" Jeffrey sat up, wishing he could see the look on Paul's face, to read his thoughts.

"Nothing, just a passing thought. Sorry I couldn't help you out. Several of the guys from Bible study go to lunch after service on Sundays. Would you like to join us?"

Jeffrey tried to think of a polite way to decline. "Sure, where at?"

"This week we're going to Cobbler Kitchen. You know it?"

"Can't say that I do. Where is it?"

Paul gave him directions and Jeffrey went into the kitchen where he found a pen and some paper. After making sure he had it all down, he hung up and left the phone on the kitchen counter.

Returning to the living room, Jeffrey flopped back on the couch, but he didn't reach for the television remote. Instead, he closed his eyes and tried to figure out what Paul had started to say. Did he wonder if Michelle would be more receptive to an invitation to church from Wendy? Had Wendy ever invited Michelle? Could he invite Michelle and Wendy to the wedding? He didn't think Stephen had a date. His mind raced in a dozen directions at once until the noise became too much.

He opened his eyes and stood up. He still wore his pajamas, a pair of thin sweatpants and a ratty t-shirt. He shed the shirt as he moved into the bedroom, where he pulled a pair of jeans from a drawer and a polo from the closet. Half an hour later he was in his truck.

He parked in front of a tired-looking diner. The letters still legible on the side of the building read "Burg-- H-ave-". Red paint peeled from wooden trim around the windows and rust threatened to consume the frame of the glass front door. Jeffrey pulled the door open and stepped inside.

A long counter ran the length of the back wall, patrons on every stool. A dozen booths lined the wall on either side of the door, with another ten tables scattered through the middle of the room. He found an empty booth at the far end of the restaurant and slipped across its torn vinyl bench. Before a server could appear, he pulled his cell phone from his pocket and thumbed in a quick message.

"Good to see you again, sugar. It's been a while." Jeffrey looked up from his phone. A tall lady in her mid-fifties with soft brown eyes, surrounded by deep laugh lines, and faded auburn hair stood over him with a warm smile.

"Too long," Jeffrey agreed. "How've you been, Wanda?"

"You know how it is. Some days are filled with smiles, others..." and she shrugged. "Bacon cheeseburger and a chocolate shake for you today?"

"How do you do it? I haven't been here in months and yet you always remember."

"I make it a point to remember the big tippers." She winked. "Back in two shakes."

Jeffrey's phone buzzed. "Hold off about ten minutes. I have a friend joining me."

"Sure thing. Want me to bring you a glass of water or a soda while you wait?"

"Water would be great, thanks." Jeffrey replied to the message with directions to the restaurant, then sat back to study the other diners.

The patrons at the counter were solitary figures, hunched over their food, looking neither left nor right, the only conversation requests for condiments. Several families with rowdy children filled the center tables, the occasional french fry being tossed from one child to another. The booths held couples; one pair even shared a large milkshake with two straws, like something out of an episode of *Happy Days*.

Jeffrey looked toward the door when he heard the hinges groan. Stephen stepped inside and Jeffrey waved. As Stephen made his way to the table, a beefy man leaned over a jukebox in the opposite corner. Jeffrey saw him punch in some numbers and heard the opening strains of "A Hard Day's Night" by the Beatles.

"Interesting choice," he mumbled as Stephen took a seat across from him.

Stephen looked down at his shirt. "What?"

"Nothing. Glad you could make it."

"I was getting ready to make a ham sandwich when I got your message. Anything sounded better than that." Stephen looked around the small restaurant. "How'd you find this place?"

"Camylle and I used to come here after her tennis matches. If she won, she treated herself to a juicy burger. If she lost, she wallowed in a banana split." The memory warmed Jeffrey.

"You don't talk about her much."

"She's been gone a long time now and I'm finally moving on."

Wanda returned with Jeffrey's burger and shake. "What can I get for you, honey?"

"Um, I haven't even looked at the menu yet." Stephen pulled one from a rack on the edge of the table.

"Bring him a cheeseburger, onion rings, and a root beer float," Jeffrey said.

Wanda glanced at Stephen. "You sure he can eat all that? He ain't no bigger than a twig."

"You'd be surprised what he can put away," Jeffrey said.

Stephen nodded and Wanda sighed. "All right, but you know how Manny feels about food left on a plate. Back in a flash."

"Your burger looks good," Stephen said.

Jeffrey lifted the half-pound monster and took a bite. "You're the only person I've ever told about this place. Except Camylle of course. A year or so after she died, I came in here and Wanda acted like I was the prodigal son, lavishing me with extra fries and super-sized shakes. When I told her about Camylle, she sat down and had a good cry, made me feel like I wasn't so alone in my grief. Since then I've come in every couple of months."

"Why'd you decide to let me in on your secret?"

"Sometimes a burger is just better when it's shared."

Wanda returned with a plate piled high with onion rings and a burger almost as large at Jeffrey's. The root beer float was served in a thirty-two-ounce glass with three scoops of ice cream. Stephen's stomach growled as if on cue, bringing a grin to Wanda's weathered face.

"Sounds like he might be up to the task after all. Anything else I can bring ya?"

"No thanks, Wanda. We're good for the time being."

Stephen bit into his burger and Jeffrey laughed when his friend's eyes rolled back in his head. "That's the best burger I've ever had," Stephen mumbled through a mouthful of food.

"I knew you'd appreciate it." Jeffrey took a long sip of his milkshake. The two ate in silence, the occasional groan of delight escaping them.

When their plates were almost empty, Jeffrey reached over to steal one of Stephen's onion rings. "Do you have a date for the wedding?"

Stephen set down his float, coughing on the carbonated drink. "What? Where did that come from?"

"I didn't know if you and Stephanie were going together or if you have another date lined up, or, well, I guess I assumed you told Lizzie you were bringing a guest."

"Stephanie and ... what do you mean? We're work friends."

"Are you sure about that? Seems like you have more in common than just work."

"We've talked a few times, after the Concierge Club dinners, and once she emailed me about a guest she had at her hotel; someone we've dealt with before at Hotel Lago."

"So you two aren't a couple and you are free to bring a date to the wedding?"

Stephen removed his glasses and polished them with the edge of his t-shirt. "I guess I could bring a date, but I told Lizzie it would be just me."

"Oh." Jeffrey used his straw to scrape at a lump of ice cream in the bottom of his glass.

"Why are you so interested?"

"I thought if you needed a date, you could bring this girl, Wendy. She's friends with Michelle. Maybe if they both came it wouldn't be so weird for Michelle to be my date."

"So I'm to be a pawn in your continued dance with Michelle? I see how you are."

"No, it's not that way." Jeffrey paused when Stephen raised an eyebrow at him. The look was something he must have learned from Lizzie. "Okay, maybe it's a little that way. Truth is, I don't know what I was thinking when I RSVP'ed with a plus one. Maybe I thought things with Michelle may have developed into something by now, but she doesn't seem at all interested in sharing my faith."

"Why's that so important to you? It's obvious you care about her, or you would have met someone else by now."

Jeffrey groaned. "If you're telling me I care about her, then I'm doomed."

"What do you mean?" Stephen looked hurt. "I may not be experienced with relationships, but I'm not blind or deaf. She's the only girl you talk about, other than Lizzie, and your face gets all soft and glowy when you talk about her."

"Glowy? Is that even a word, and I don't get glowy."

"Word or not, it's what happens to you. You had the same look when you were talking about Camylle earlier."

"Then it's a good thing I haven't asked Michelle to the wedding. She probably sees my glowy face and thinks I'm pining away for her. That has to stop, today."

"How do you propose to do that? Stop seeing her altogether?"

"If that's what I have to do, yes. I can't wrap myself up in a relationship that doesn't have God at its center."

"Are you sure she won't come to believe in God if you were to start dating, for real I mean. No more of this arm's length stuff."

"Listen to you. You sound like Ian. I liked you better when you were just Stephen: clueless and quiet."

"I'm sorry. Maybe I should leave." Stephen pulled his wallet from his pocket and fumbled with several bills. "How much do you think my meal was?"

Jeffrey reached across the table and pushed the bills back into Stephen's wallet. "Forget about it. I'm sorry I said that. I didn't mean it in a bad way."

"Sure, there are plenty of good things about 'clueless and quiet'." Stephen slid to the outside of the booth.

"Stephen, wait," Jeffrey called, but the door was already slamming shut.

CHAPTER TWENTY-SIX

Ian parked in front of the restaurant and opened the car door for his mother, his gaze slipping through the parking lot toward the entrance, in search of Lizzie. Colin and Cassandra followed him through the front door where a hostess greeted them with a welcoming smile.

"We are meeting someone," Ian said, scanning the tables.

"An attractive blonde?"

Ian nodded and the hostess led them past a dozen tables and around a corner, where Lizzie sat waiting. She stood when they approached and Ian pulled her into his arms. She smelled sweet and clean, like she'd come from a bath in a candy store.

"All right, let someone else have a turn," Colin teased. Ian gave Lizzie a squeeze before letting her go, so she could be enveloped by Colin and Cassandra in turn.

"It's so good to see you," Cassandra said. "You look beautiful. I love what you've done with your hair."

"Thank you," Lizzie said. Ian noticed the faint flush of color to her cheeks.

When they were all seated and orders had been placed, Lizzie turned to Cassandra and Colin. "Is your room at the hotel okay?"

"It's marvelous," Cassandra said.

"I hope the front desk staff told you all about the concierge lounge too."

"Stephen was there and he took care of them," Ian said.

"He was? I thought he was off today." Lizzie's brow furrowed.

Ian wondered if the young assistant manager had only come in to make sure his parents were taken care of properly. It seemed like the type of thing Stephen would do to impress Lizzie.

"Ian said you had a dress fitting today," Cassandra said. "How did it go?"

"I need to go back next week for another fitting of my gown." She turned to Ian. "I lost a few more pounds than I thought when I had the flu."

"I'm not surprised. You've hardly eaten all week."

"Would you mind if I went with you to the next fitting?" Cassandra asked. Ian could see the hope in his mother's eyes but sensed Lizzie stiffen beside him.

Colin reached for his wife's hand. "Cassie, maybe she wants everyone to see the dress for the first time at the ceremony."

Ian heard Lizzie exhale and met his father's gaze, giving Colin a minute nod of thanks.

"I haven't scheduled the appointment yet, but I can let you know when I do," Lizzie said, a tiny tremor in her voice.

When his mother smiled, Ian half expected patrons at the front of the restaurant to ask why the room had become so bright.

"The flowers in our suite are lovely. Stephen mentioned the same florist is doing your wedding flowers." Cassandra took a sip of her water.

"Jackson is amazing. I was having a hard time narrowing down which flowers I wanted to use, but he was able to understand my vision even before I did."

"These two could talk wedding plans all night," Colin said.

Cassandra swatted at his arm. "We are here for their wedding."

"Are you going to visit any of the attractions while you are in town?" Lizzie said. "There's plenty of time between now and the wedding and the theme parks are beautifully decorated for the holiday."

Colin frowned. "We aren't much into theme parks."

"There are plenty of other things to keep you busy. There's a winery about thirty minutes away, there are several museums, and Winter Park has some great shopping."

"I wish we could take some time off to show you around," Ian said.

"We'll be fine." Colin leaned back so the server could pass out the plates that had arrived. "We'll rent a car tomorrow and do some exploring."

"But we'll only be a phone call away if you need any help with the wedding," Cassandra added.

Ian felt Lizzie tense again and placed a reassuring hand on her shoulder. "I told you, Lizzie has everything under control. This isn't the first wedding she's planned."

"Well, I could use some help with the place cards for the reception. Stephanie, Emma and I were going to work on them tomorrow night."

"Just tell me where and when and I'll be there." Ian half expected his mother to clap her hands in delight.

"How's business, dad?" Ian reached for his knife and cut spears of asparagus into bite size pieces.

"Things are good. We always slow down this time of year. Everyone is busy preparing for Christmas."

"Same here. I have one more design to finish before the wedding then I'm free until January."

"You do have clients lined up for the new year, though, right?" Cassandra frowned, her concern evident to Ian.

"Of course. There are two banks finalizing land deals now that I will be meeting with after we return from our honeymoon." He couldn't help giving Lizzie a mischievous grin.

Cassandra relaxed and cut into her filet mignon. "Are you finally going to tell us what your plans for the honeymoon are?"

"Nope, it's going to be a surprise to all."

Lizzie's lower lip poked out in a pout that made Ian chuckle. "How am I supposed to know what to pack?"

"You can pack one bag for warm weather and one for cold, or maybe I'll pack for you. I like that idea even better."

"Will I need a passport? I'm not sure if mine is up to date or not."

"It is. I found it while you were sick. You still have two years before it needs to be renewed."

"Ah-ha!" Triumph danced in Lizzie's eyes. "So we're going somewhere outside the country."

Ian shrugged. "Maybe, or maybe I just like to have all my bases covered."

Lizzie stuck out her tongue at him. "You haven't been making me practice twirling my pasta on a fork, so we must not be going to Italy."

"If all those dinners at Tramonti with Arnaldo chiding you for cutting your pasta hasn't broken you of that habit, then nothing will."

"Is that the Arnaldo you were telling me about who offers the wine seminars?" Colin said.

Ian nodded and swallowed the bite of fish he'd taken. "Lizzie and I go to his restaurant a couple of times a month. We'll take you for dinner one night while you're here."

"Our time will fill up before we know it," Colin said. "Lizzie, are you taking any time off before the wedding?"

"No, we have a lot going on this month. Several of our most frequent guests will be arriving and I have a meeting with one of our larger corporate groups to plan their retreat for next year."

"Don't you have a convention manager for those things? I thought you were the concierge manager," Cassandra said.

"We've had several temporary convention mangers over the past six months, but I've done the majority of the planning. Melvin is our current manager and he is ... useless is a bit harsh, maybe unprepared is the best way to put it."

"That's terrible. Why hasn't someone more qualified been hired?"

"There are a number of factors, our wedding being one," Ian said. "Lizzie's the natural choice for the job, but she's too conscientious to take it, then leave it unattended for two weeks while we're on our honeymoon."

"Melvin may not be ideal, but he is an extra body who can help Stephen out while I'm gone. Stephen will have his hands full managing the concierge and keeping Melvin in line, but he can handle it."

"He seemed quite capable and dedicated when we met him this afternoon," Colin said.

"I could never have agreed to such a long trip if I didn't have Stephen in the office."

"Remind me to thank him again." Ian grinned and leaned over to drop a kiss on Lizzie's cheek.

CHAPTER TWENTY-SEVEN

"You want me to pick you up for church in the morning?" Ian asked as he walked Lizzie to his car.

"Only if that means I can have my own car back. I've been terrified I might wreck yours."

"Thank you for inviting mom to help with the place cards. She wants to help any way she can."

"Doesn't she have her hands full planning the rehearsal dinner? I gave her a list of places she might want to have it. Chef even offered to hold it at the hotel, but I never heard back from her."

"I don't know. I thought she was working with you on it. I'll talk to her on the way to the hotel, but you don't need to worry about it." He kissed her forehead and pulled her close.

"Our banquet rooms are booked up now, but if we don't have too large a party, I can probably get us a reservation in the restaurant, but I need to know soon."

"What did I just say? Don't worry about it. There's not much the groom's side has to worry about. Mom and I will take care of it." He felt her tremble and looked down into her eyes, which glistened with unshed tears.

"I miss my mom," she whispered before burying her face in his chest.

"I know, baby. I can't imagine how much it must hurt and I wish I could take away the pain."

Lizzie sniffed and stepped back. "You better get back to your parents. They must be tired from traveling."

Ian didn't want to let her go, but he knew she'd closed the door on the pain that had crept forward. He'd seen her do it too many times in the past months. He prayed one day she'd let him in to share her sorrow.

"I'll see you in the morning." He kissed her then stepped back and waited for her to duck into the car. When she pulled out of the parking space, he turned and made his way to the car where his parents were waiting.

"Is everything all right?" Cassandra asked when Ian started the car.

"She's worried about the rehearsal dinner. I thought you were working with her to plan it."

"She has so much going on already."

"But you do have it planned, right?"

"I've talked with a couple of places."

Ian turned to face his mother in the backseat. "You don't have anything reserved yet?"

"I thought once we got down here it would be easier to visit the places and see what feels like the best fit."

"Oh, mom." He sighed and turned back around to hide his disappointment. "Why didn't you tell me? I could have gone to any of the places you were interested in. Reservations are hard to get this time of year."

"This is the one thing the mother of the groom gets to plan. I wanted to do the actual planning, not delegate it to you or Lizzie."

"You need to nail it down soon, as in by Monday."

"As soon as we get the rental car tomorrow we'll take care of it," Colin assured him.

Ian returned his parents to the hotel and thought about going to Lizzie's house, exchanging the cars now instead of tomorrow, but something held him back. Instead, he reached for his cell phone and dialed a number.

"Emma, it's Ian."

"How are you doing, Ian? Did your folks get in okay?"

"They did, thanks. I was wondering if you'd mind checking on Lizzie for me. I think she might need you tonight."

"What's the matter?" Emma's maternal instinct made Ian believe he'd been right to call her.

"Dinner with my parents was hard for her. I would go over, but I'm not sure I'm what she needs right now."

"I'll give her a call as soon as we hang up. You're a good man to understand the way you do."

"Thanks, Emma." Ian hung up and pulled out of the hotel lot. Lizzie would be in good hands.

CHAPTER TWENTY-EIGHT

The front window of the Loaded Hog glowed with Christmas lights wrapped around an inflatable palm tree and a picture of Santa Claus in a bathing suit. Michelle shook her head when she saw the display as she entered the crowded club. She elbowed her way to the bar and signaled the bartender.

"Hey, Jimmy."

"Hey, what are you doing here? I thought you guys were playing at The Social again tonight." The bartender wiped away a water ring near Michelle's elbow.

"We are. I thought I'd come in for a drink to settle my nerves. There's a rumor a talent agent is in town and has been hitting the clubs all week. I wish I'd never heard about him so I could play our normal show without any nerves."

"You've been getting some great gigs, and since Tina split, your whole sound has improved. That girl was holding you all back." Jimmy reached under the bar for a glass and started pouring. "Gin martini with three olives, right?"

"Thanks." Michelle brushed hair off her forehead and looked over her shoulder at the audience building behind her. "Who's playing tonight? They must be popular to have this kind of crowd."

Jimmy handed her a glass. "A group from Jacksonville. I think they're called *Sour Grapes* or something like that. The manager saw them up there a couple of months ago and has been trying to get them in here ever since. They're supposed to sound like *Dashboard Confessional.*"

"They came from Jacksonville to play here?"

"Don't make it sound like this is such a dump."

"Sorry, it's just a long drive to play a couple of hours."

"Maybe they heard about the talent scout too."

Michelle cocked her head at the sound of an amp being turned on. A couple of scrawny guys in tight jeans and black tank tops with guitars slung low over their hips took the stage. She saw movement behind the drums as well, but couldn't make out anything more than a thick head of black hair and pale skin.

She listened to the first two songs, sipping on her martini. Jimmy had moved down the bar to take care of other customers, leaving her alone to critique the band. They didn't have the understated elegance of *Dashboard*; they struck her more as a screaming *Blink-182* cover band. Satisfied they didn't pose any real competition to her own *Tangled Web*, she knocked on the bar to get Jimmy's attention.

"What do you think?" he asked, flipping his bar towel over his shoulder.

"Not my style, but it might explain why the manager here never wanted to give us better show times."

"You may be right. I had no idea Gary had such bad taste in music. I hope this is the only night these guys are available to play, otherwise I might have to look for another job."

"I can put in a good word for you at The Social." Michelle smiled and tucked a piece of hair behind her ear.

"I'm off at eleven tonight. You want to get a drink after your show?"

The invitation surprised Michelle. She'd known Jimmy for three years but they'd never seen each other outside the Loaded Hog, him behind the bar, her on the stage. An image of Jeffrey flitted through her mind, followed by Wendy's question about Michelle dating anyone. "Sure, why not. Meet you at Back Booth around midnight?"

"Sounds good. Knock 'em dead tonight."

Michelle watched Jimmy move down the bar, checking on customers and pouring fresh drinks while she finished off her own. She caught him look her way and smile, displaying a row of perfect white teeth, sending a tiny shiver down her spine. She gave a little wave, then turned with a flip of her hair, and weaved out of the throbbing crowd.

She walked down Orange Avenue toward a small parking lot where she'd left her guitar in the trunk of her car. Bemused by Jimmy's interest, she was oblivious to the cacophony of battling bands and car stereos. As she unlocked her car and pulled the guitar case out, she felt a hand on her shoulder and spun around.

"Michelle, are you all right?"

"Matt, you scared me to death."

"I've been calling your name for the past two blocks. Didn't you hear me?"

"I must have been distracted." She looked around but didn't see Matt's drum case. "Are you already set up inside?"

"No, that's what I've been trying to tell you. We've been bumped."

"What? They can't do that."

Matt shrugged. "They just did. The club owner told me he'd booked a band who're only in town for the night. The *Sour Apples* or something. I've never heard of them."

"Are you kidding me? They're playing the Loaded Hog right now."

"How's that possible? I saw the stage at The Social already set up for them."

"What time are they supposed to go on?"

"I assume ten, like we were scheduled to."

"No way they can play an hour and a half at the Loaded Hog then bounce over to The Social and play another two hours. Come on."

"Where are we going?"

"To get our gig back."

CHAPTER TWENTY-NINE

A greasy-haired lump of a man who chewed on the stub of a cigar met Michelle at the back door to the club. He reeked of sweat and smoke, his face covered with two days of stubble that did little to cover his acne scars. "Look, I already told your drummer, I have another group coming in tonight."

"Lenny, I know what you told Matt, but did you know your replacement band is currently playing at the Loaded Hog? I can't imagine they have enough material in their scrawny little heads to provide two unique shows. The crowds that usually come in here will have already heard them. They'll hit the bricks by the time the second song starts. Sure, you'll get some of the later arrivals, but the place won't be as packed as it is when we play. People are coming out to see *Tangled Web*, not some crappy cover band."

"They aren't a cover band. They have original music."

"What I just heard at the Hog could have come off any *Blink-182* album. The words may have been different, but the sound's the same. Do you want to get a reputation for dissing your regulars in favor of a bunch of posers?"

"One night doesn't make a reputation. You guys'll be back on stage next weekend."

"Your call, but I can tell you, word will be out on our website before the end of the night. Maybe I will even talk to one of the legal guys in the office Monday about drawing up some performance contracts for us to use in the future."

"Michelle, come on. We're friends aren't we?"

"I thought we might be, Lenny, but now, I don't know if I want friends like you. Come on, Matt, we need to update the website." Michelle turned on her heel and started toward the street.

"Wait! Come back. You win."

Michelle gave Matt a tiny smile before turning back around. "I'm so happy to hear that, Lenny. We'll need you to tear down their equipment while we get ready."

"I can't do..." but Lenny stopped when Michelle stepped back toward the sidewalk again. "All right. I'll get a couple of guys to gather up their equipment. Come on in."

"I'll be back with my drums in five minutes." Matt scampered down the alley and disappeared around the corner.

Michelle leaned close to Lenny. "Don't try to pull something like this again or I will make sure every band in town knows you can't be trusted."

Lenny nodded and tossed his cigar stub into a nearby garbage can. "Can I get you something to drink before you go on?"

"A bottle of water would be great. Thanks." She gave him a sweet smile and rested her guitar case against the wall.

Matt returned a few minutes later, followed by their bass player, Jonesy, and the newest member of the band, Aimee, who played keyboard.

"Matt told us we were bumped but you got us back in," Aimee whispered, her eyes wide with awe.

"If there's a talent scout in town tonight, no one is getting in my way."

"You think we're good enough for a scout to notice us?" Jonesy looked skeptical.

"I think we are, but we all need to believe that. If you have doubts then we won't have a shot. Think about the gigs we're playing now compared to a year ago. Don't you think we're better?"

Jonesy gave a hesitant nod. "I hate to admit it, but since Tina left we have become more popular. We have over a thousand fans online now."

"Opening for *Wonderland* was our first break, gave us visibility to a whole new audience. Tonight we are going to get our next break, and maybe even a record deal." She could feel the other band members catching her excitement, could see in their eyes the flash of desire. "So are we going to make this our best show yet?"

They all cheered. "I'm glad I stuck with you when Tina split." Jonesy slung an arm around Michelle's shoulders and kissed the side of her head.

"Now let's get ready to rock this place."

Lenny returned with Michelle's bottled water, his eyes shifting from her to the door.

"Don't worry, Lenny. If those *Sour Grapes*, *Apples*, whoever they are, give you a hard time, tell them I stormed the stage." She gulped down half the bottle of water before stepping out onto the stage and taking the microphone from a server who was getting ready to announce the band.

"Hello, Orlando! We are *Tangled Web*. Are you ready to party?"

The crowd went wild and the band set off on a heart-pounding song Michelle had written the previous month. Her eyes never left the crowd, searching for anyone who stood out as a talent scout. She expected it to be a man in an expensive suit, sitting back by the bar where he'd have a good view of the crowd and the band. There appeared to be no one fitting this description anywhere in the club, but she kept up her act of bravado.

Two hours later, she stepped off the stage after a double encore, the crowd still shouting for more. She slipped the guitar strap over her shoulder and rested the instrument in its case.

"That was quite a show."

She turned and felt her pulse rise even higher than the adrenaline from the show had already taken it. "Andy, it's good to see you. I thought you were out on the road."

"We have a two week break and I missed home. There's been a lot of buzz about the talent in Orlando, especially a group called *Tangled Web*." His green eyes rested on her and she remembered the first time they'd met. She'd taken Jeffrey and Ian to see *Wonderland* play, and after the show she'd had a chance to talk to Andy. When he heard she was a musician as well, he'd insisted on knowing when her next show was, so he could attend. That had been the last time she'd seen Jeffrey until after Amanda's murder. Why did Jeffrey keep coming up in her memories?

"Don't tease me. We're just a local group trying to get a steady gig," she said.

"That's not the word on the street. Rumor has it a talent agent is in town specifically to see you guys."

"Well, I didn't see anyone who looked like a scout tonight. We did have a great show, though, didn't we?"

"The best yet. You want to get a drink?"

"I wish I could, but," Michelle checked her watch, "I'm supposed to be meeting someone in a couple of minutes."

"I should've known you'd have a fella waiting for you. Maybe we can grab lunch this week. I'm in town until the tenth and then we hit the road again."

"You won't be home for Christmas?"

Some of the light left Andy's eyes and he shook his head. "There are sacrifices that come with a record deal. You still have my number?"

"I'll give you a call tomorrow afternoon."

"All right. Have fun tonight." He gave her a hug and disappeared into the crowd.

"Was that Andy from *Wonderland*?" Aimee gasped.

"Yeah, I'm sorry I didn't introduce you. I forget you haven't been with us all along. He's a good guy."

"He's gorgeous, and so talented. He and I would make the most beautiful, musical babies."

Michelle guffawed and slung the guitar case over her shoulder. "I doubt you're the first woman to think that, Aimee."

"Wasn't he dating some local actress, Julia Keen, I think her name was?"

"Now that's one gorgeous woman," Matt joined in. "Legs for miles and eyes the color of the Caribbean Sea. They broke up six months ago."

Michelle looked at Matt. "How do you know that?"

"She didn't like that his career was taking off and hers wasn't. Sure, she was well known here in town, but Hollywood hasn't been knocking down her door. They had a big blowout at Hue. I have a friend who works there, told me all about it."

"I hate to play and run, but I have to be someplace. Are you guys going to hang out a while?"

"I don't think I'll be able to sleep for days," Jonesy said. "If anyone wants to hit a couple of clubs, I'm game." Matt and Aimee nodded.

"Maybe I'll see you guys later then. Have fun; it was a great show." Michelle pushed through the back door and hurried to her car to stow her guitar. At ten minutes past midnight she dropped into a chair at Back Booth where Jimmy was waiting.

CHAPTER THIRTY

"I take it your show went well?" Jimmy leaned forward so he could be heard over the band on stage.

Michelle nodded and waved to a server. "Can I get a bottle of water and dirty martini please?"

"I'll take another beer, too, please," Jimmy added. "I was going to try to catch your show, but the boss asked me to help restock the beer cooler before I left."

Michelle glanced at his biceps, stretching the fabric of his black t-shirt. He was certainly built for heavy lifting, she thought. "I think it was our best show yet, but I didn't see anyone who looked like a talent scout."

"They don't stick out as much as you might think. I tended bar at a couple of clubs in Nashville. The scouts looked like everyone else, but they'd talk to me, ask about the bands, how the crowds reacted to them, how long they'd been playing."

The server returned with their drinks and Michelle downed the bottle of water. "I didn't know you were from Nashville. What brought you to Florida?"

"I'm from Florida. I went to Nashville hoping to get a record deal. I tended bar to pay the rent, but I played every chance I got. A few of the scouts I met while behind the bar saw me play as well. One of them was kind enough to tell me I didn't have the 'it' factor they were looking for. Six months later, I packed up and came home."

Michelle studied him, trying to figure out what he was missing. At six foot two, with muscles in all the right places and brown eyes that could melt the heart of the most bitter woman, Jimmy appeared to exude the "it" factor. "If they didn't think you could make it, there's no chance for *Tangled Web*. We look like a bunch of gutter rats next to you."

Jimmy's laugh made the hair on Michelle's neck tingle. "I would never call you a gutter rat. Jonesy, maybe, but not you. I don't think my looks were the problem, though. I love music and I loved playing, but I never had the burning passion you have. *That's* what the scouts are looking for."

She shifted in her seat, the intimate look in Jimmy's eyes drawing her in. He leaned closer and she could smell his aftershave over the normal bar odors. It made her think of a regal stag emerging from a cedar forest.

"You have the 'it' factor, Michelle. The scouts will find you." He was so close she could feel his breath on her neck. She turned to face him, and without hesitation, he closed the distance between them, meeting her lips.

She fell into his kiss, savoring the taste of beer and salt. The sound of the band on stage was soon drowned out by the pounding of her heart. Jimmy pulled her closer, his hand twisting in her thick hair.

"You want to get out of here?" he whispered in between kisses.

Michelle moaned as his lips moved down her neck. Her forehead tingled and she touched a small scar above her eye. Like a shock from a defibrillator, she jolted to her senses and gently pushed Jimmy back.

"I like you, Jimmy, but I can't do this." She moved her chair back, trying to put some distance between them, willing her heart to slow.

"I'm sorry," he said, and scooted back as well, putting the table between them. "I've wanted to do that for a long time and..." He looked at the floor for a long minute.

"It was nice," Michelle said, "but I have some stuff going on right now. I'm not sure –"

"Forget about it. I was caught up in the moment. It won't happen again." He stood and placed a twenty-dollar bill on the table. "That should cover the drinks."

Michelle watched him leave, wondering why she had stopped him, why her scar had chosen that moment to remind her of past mistakes. She heard an echo of the words Jeffrey had spoken several months before. *"Until you can see me without thinking of whatever that scar represents, you won't trust me completely."*

"Why can't I get you out of my head?" she growled. Her martini sat on the table, untouched. She looked at the glass, wondering how many it would take to silence her memories.

CHAPTER THIRTY-ONE

Jeffrey lay awake in bed, watching the ceiling fan whirr above him. The thin sheet felt scratchy against his skin, but he kept it around him like a protective cocoon. After Stephen had stormed out of the diner, Jeffrey had tried to call him, but the calls had gone straight to voicemail.

For the first time in months, he'd craved a drink and had started to call Wally a dozen times during the evening. One night at the bar wouldn't hurt him, would it? He knew calling Lizzie would have been the right move, but he hadn't wanted to talk about why he needed a drink. He couldn't tell Lizzie he'd upset Stephen. So, he'd taken a long, cold shower, and tried to read a C. S. Lewis book Lizzie had given him. Finally, he'd given up and crawled into bed, but sleep didn't come.

His phone rang, startling him. He answered without looking at the caller ID, his gaze transfixed on the fan. "Hello?"

"Why don't you want to take me to Lizzie's wedding?"

"What? Michelle, is that you?" He pulled the sheet back and sat up, glancing at the clock. The red display showed one thirty in the morning.

"You've been trying to get me to meet her for a year, but now you won't even ask me to be your date at her wedding. Are you afraid I will embarrass you?"

"Michelle, where are you? Are you okay?" Jeffrey could hear music and cars in the background and wondered if she was downtown. He tried to remember if she'd had a show.

"Answer me!"

"Maybe we should talk about this in the morning. You sound—"

"What? I sound like I've been drinking? You should know, shouldn't you?"

Jeffrey felt a stab in his heart. "Where are you? I'm coming to get you." He stood, pulled on a pair of pants and retrieved a t-shirt from the rim of his laundry hamper.

"Don't bother. I can take care of myself."

"Are you with the band? Can I talk to Matt or Jonesy?"

"No, I'm not with them. I can have my own life too. There are other guys who find me desirable."

Jeffrey grabbed his keys off the coffee table and charged out the door. "Of course you're desirable. You're beautiful *and* talented."

He started the truck and backed out of the driveway. He hoped, if he could keep her on the phone, he'd be able to find out where she was by the time he reached downtown.

"Then why don't you want me?" Her anger was turning to tears.

"Oh, Michelle, it's not like that at all. I'm on my way, tell me where you are."

"You had your chance. Now it's someone else's turn."

The line went dead and Jeffrey pushed the accelerator even harder, praying there were no police in the area. He knew he had to get to Michelle before it was too late. He maneuvered off I-4 and cruised down Orange Avenue, scanning the sidewalks for Michelle. He didn't know how he'd find her in the crush of people flowing from one club to another.

"Dear Lord, show me the way. Lead me to her." He turned into a parking garage and found a spot on the first level then jumped out and ran to the sidewalk. He looked left and right, orienting himself, then plunged into the crowd, headed toward Wall Street Cantina. He dialed Michelle's number, hoping he'd hear it ringing in the crowd or that she'd answer and he'd be able to recognize the background noise.

He weaved through the throngs loitering outside the Cantina and emerged on the other side of the courtyard. The light faded as he moved away from the bars toward the History Center.

"What's the matter, little lady? Let me dry those tears." Jeffrey heard the voice then muffled sobs from somewhere to his left. He saw a figure crouched close to the ground and another leaning over it.

"Michelle?" he called, running toward the dark forms. The standing figure straightened, then moved off in the opposite direction.

Jeffrey found Michelle sitting on a rock, arms wrapped around her knees, head buried in her lap, sobbing. He knelt beside her and placed a hand on her shoulder. She flinched, turning her body away from him, but not looking up.

"Michelle, it's okay. I'm here," he coaxed.

She lifted her head and met his gaze. "Why did you come?"

"I was worried about you. It's late. Let me take you home." He extended a hand, but she looked away.

"I haven't been drinking."

"That's good to hear, but I still think you need to go home. We can talk about this later, after you've had some sleep."

"I don't need sleep to know you've turned my life upside down. I've been going to church for months, but it was all head knowledge until tonight. Now, I don't know what I believe."

Jeffrey froze. She'd been going to church? Why wouldn't she tell me? "Shh, it's going to be all right. Come on, I'll walk you to your car."

This time she took his offered hand and stood up. He pulled her into his arms and held her while she cried. When her tears seemed spent, he leaned back so he could see her face. Her eyes were red and swollen. He wiped away the trace of tears with his thumbs, clasping her head in his palms. She looked heartbreakingly vulnerable.

"Would you mind driving me home?"

"Not at all." He grinned and slipped his hand in hers.

The ride was silent except for her directions when a turn was needed. Jeffrey spent the time praying for guidance for himself and peace for Michelle.

"Here we are," she said, pointing to an apartment complex. Jeffrey turned in and followed her directions to a parking spot.

He cut the engine and turned to her. "Get some sleep and I'll call you this afternoon. We have a lot to talk about."

She nodded and descended from the truck. He watched her climb a flight of stairs and waited until he saw her front door close before resting his head on the steering wheel and releasing a thankful sigh.

CHAPTER THIRTY-TWO

Clouds skidded across the sky as Jeffrey emerged from the church service. After leaving Michelle at her apartment, it had taken him hours to fall asleep. As a result he'd only gotten an hour of rest before his alarm went off. He'd considered silencing it and skipping church, but his conscience pulled him out of bed. Now he was glad he'd come. While still exhausted, he felt fortified and ready to have a serious talk with Michelle. He saw Paul with a group of guys he recognized from the Wednesday Bible study.

Jeffrey tapped Paul on the shoulder. "Hey, can I talk to you for a second?"

Paul stepped away from the group. "You still coming to lunch?"

"No, something came up last night that I need to take care of."

"Everything okay?"

"I'm not sure."

"Give me a second." Paul turned back to the group. "I'll meet you guys at the restaurant. You know what to order for me."

"I don't want to take you away from lunch, I just wanted to let you know I can't make it."

"Walk with me." Paul moved back toward the church. "Tell me what happened."

"It's Michelle. She called last night from a club and, well, she dropped some bombshells on me."

"Such as?"

"She told me she's been going to church and that I've turned her life upside down. To be honest, she wasn't making much sense. I thought she was drunk and I went downtown to look for her, but when I found her she appeared sober. I'm worried about her, though. Some of the things she said…" Jeffrey shook his head.

"I take it you're going to see her now."

"I need to call and see where she wants to meet."

"You want some back up?"

"I appreciate the offer, but I don't want her to think I'm ganging up on her. You could pray for me, though. I have no idea what to say to her."

Paul nodded. "Do you mind if I ask the guys to pray as well? I won't tell them the whole story, just that you are in need of prayer today."

"You'd do that?"

"Sure, that's what fellowship is about. We support each other and we lift each other up. Even if we don't know the whole story, God does, and He will meet the needs."

For the first time Jeffrey understood what Lizzie and Ian had been trying to tell him about the importance of getting involved with other believers. The idea that these guys would pray for him after meeting him only once was overwhelming. "I'd appreciate it. Thanks."

"Call me later; let me know how it goes?"

Jeffrey nodded.

"I'll let you get to it then. God be with you."

Jeffrey leaned against the church wall and pulled his cell phone from his pocket. He had a missed text message from Michelle.

Sorry about last night. Can we just forget it ever happened?

He texted back. *We need to talk. Where do you want to meet?*

He waited five minutes without a reply, then punched in her number and waited as the phone rang. It went to voicemail. Shoving the phone into his pocket, he strode across the parking lot and jumped into his truck.

He arrived at her apartment complex twenty-five minutes later, parking in the same spot as the previous night, and studied the doors on the second floor, trying to remember which one Michelle had entered. When he felt certain he had the right door, he took the stairs two at a time.

He could hear the television through the front door before he knocked. It went silent but she didn't come to the door. He knocked again. "Michelle, I know you're home."

Another minute passed before the door opened. "Do we have to do this now?"

"I think we do. Are you going to let me in, or do you want to get dressed and go someplace public?"

She stepped back and opened the door wider. "Come in."

She wore a baggy t-shirt and a pair of flannel shorts. Dark circles rimmed her eyes and Jeffrey wondered if she'd gotten any sleep. She took a seat on the couch and he closed the door behind him. His eyes swept around the room, taking in the bookcases and their few framed photos mixed in with several popular novels he recognized. On the desk in the corner, he noticed a computer monitor, a postcard taped to the side of the screen. The postcard had a church on the front, but he didn't recognize the name. He wondered if that was where she'd been going.

She broke the silence by asking, "Did you get any sleep?"

"An hour or so, you?"

She shrugged.

The couch was the only seating in the living room, so Jeffrey reached for one of the dining room chairs and set it across from Michelle. "What happened last night?"

"I was confused and upset. I shouldn't have called you."

"Why were you so upset that I didn't ask you to go to the wedding? You've made it clear you don't want to meet Lizzie."

"But you didn't even ask me."

"We aren't dating, Michelle. You aren't my girlfriend and I didn't want to confuse the situation by asking you to be my date."

"Are you dating anyone?"

"You know I'm not."

"How do I know that? As you said, we aren't dating; we don't even talk that much. You could have a whole life I don't know about."

Jeffrey placed his hands on his knees and leaned forward. "You're right. We both could have lives the other knows nothing about, but I've been completely honest with you. Other than the day-to-day of my job, you know everything that's happened in my life for the past year. You, on the other hand, have a secret life. Do you want to tell me about the church you've been going to?"

Michelle stretched her t-shirt out, and pulled her knees up under it. "Yeah, I've been going to church for a couple of months and doing research online. There is sufficient evidence to make me believe there was a man named Jesus who was crucified."

Jeffrey felt his pulse quicken. Could it be true that she had become a believer? Could he let down the wall he'd built between them?

"Beyond that, I don't know what I believe."

Jeffrey's hopes deflated. "You don't believe in the resurrection of Jesus?"

"It seems impossible, but I also don't know how to reconcile so many accounts of people from that era proclaiming his resurrection to the point of their own death. Even now I've found reports of people doing the same despite having a gun to their head. I think I'd deny my own name if that would save my life."

Jeffrey closed his eyes, wishing Paul or Lizzie were here with him. He didn't know how to transfer the intellectual understanding into a heart understanding. His own transformation had come in his heart before he'd truly understood it in his mind.

"What happened last night to make you call me?"

Jeffrey watched as Michelle's eyes grew distant. He wondered what she was thinking, what she might be reliving. Her hand moved to the scar above her eye.

"Did someone hurt you?" He reached for her hand and clasped it in both of his.

"No, I think he wanted to love me."

CHAPTER THIRTY-THREE

Michelle pulled her hands free of Jeffrey's and crossed her arms in front of her chest. She'd seen hope flare in his eyes when she'd said she believed Jesus had been a real person. She had also seen it flicker out when she'd admitted she wasn't sure she believed in the resurrection. She'd expected him to come at her with some argument to convince her, but instead he changed the subject.

"So you are dating someone else? That's good." Jeffrey leaned back in the chair and crossed his legs. "I'm happy for you."

"No, we aren't dating, but I realized last night that he's liked me for a long time." Michelle tried to remember when she'd met Jimmy, but no memory stood out. He'd always been behind the bar when she was on stage and he'd always had a bottle of water ready for her when she finished a show. Sometimes she'd hang out at the bar after her set, to check out other acts, and he'd come talk to her between serving other customers.

"Is that a bad thing?" Jeffrey crossed his arms before his chest. She felt like he was putting as much distance between them as he could without moving his chair.

"It's surprising."

"Why? You're attractive, funny, confident. I'm sure there are plenty of guys out there who like you but are too afraid to do anything about it."

Michelle snorted. "I've never known a guy to be afraid of me. I have more experience with those who want me to be afraid of them." She reached for the scar above her eye, but stopped when she noticed Jeffrey's gaze trained on it.

"You were going to touch your scar. He must have done a real number on you."

"Yeah, he did. I thought keeping the scar would prevent me from making the same mistake, but it seems to be keeping me from moving on."

"You want to talk about it?" Jeffrey uncrossed his arms and leaned forward a fraction. In response, Michelle wrapped her arms around her knees and pulled them closer to her body.

"I've had a couple of bad relationships," Michelle whispered. "One guy nearly beat me to death, and another, well, I went through the windshield of his car. That's where the scar comes from. My face was pretty cut up, but I asked the plastic surgeon to leave this scar. He did a great job. Most people don't notice it, but I always know it's there."

She thought she saw Jeffrey smile, but in an instant it was gone. He leaned a little closer, though, and his eyes compelled her to meet his.

"Scars are interesting things. They can have funny stories, like this one." He rolled up the leg of his pants and pointed at a faint scar on his shin. "I got this when I was playing hide-and-go-seek with some neighbors. I ran past a rusty paint can and got a nasty cut." He let the leg of his pants down again.

"Some have darker memories, like yours, and some memorialize the greatest sacrifice ever made. You've done your research so you know the accounts of those who saw Jesus after he rose from the dead, those who mentioned the scars on his hands, feet, and side. He is the Son of God. Don't you think He could have healed those scars and had a perfect body again?"

Michelle shrugged. "Sure, but then how could He prove He was the same man they had hung on the cross. Maybe there was an unknown twin brother."

Now there was no question Jeffrey was smiling. It was so wide she thought she could see his molars. "His scars are proof of His sacrifice and a reminder to us of His love."

Michelle released her knees and stretched her legs. "I see what you did there."

"What?" His eyebrows shot up in surprise.

"You got me to admit Jesus had to have come back from the dead."

"Did I? All I heard you say was that the scars proved He was the same man who was crucified, not a twin who'd been in hiding all along."

"Stop it, you won." She sighed.

"This isn't a battle, Michelle." He paused and looked her in the eyes. "Well, in a way it is, but not between you and me. The battle is between you and God."

She stood up and walked around the back of the couch, and studied the bookcase, but didn't register any of the items on its shelves. If Jesus rose from the dead, then everything else had to be true, which meant there was life after death, heaven and hell; there was freedom and peace available to those who believed; there was forgiveness.

Her back stiffened as she remembered something she'd read about forgiveness, something she'd heard for years when people would recite the Lord's Prayer at weddings or funerals. "Forgive us our sins as we forgive those who sin against us."

"What did you say?"

She turned, unaware she'd said the words out loud. "Part of the Lord's Prayer; forgive us our sins as we forgive those who sin against us. I don't know if I can forgive those guys who abused me."

"Forgiving is hard. Sometimes the hurt is so deep we can't forgive on our own, but God can heal our deepest hurts and give us that strength, give us the desire to forgive, to let go of the bitterness."

Michelle returned to the couch and dropped down on it. "I'm tired. Can we talk about this later?"

Jeffrey leaned forward, elbows on his knees, his face close to hers. "If you aren't comfortable talking to me about all the things you are thinking, call Wendy. I'm sure if she can't answer your questions she knows another woman who can. I understand you don't want to talk to Lizzie, but maybe you do need the support of other women."

He stood and returned the chair to its place at the table. "I'm only a phone call away."

CHAPTER THIRTY-FOUR

"Thanks so much for coming over, Stephanie." Lizzie set a cardboard box on the dining room table and pulled out a chair next to Emma.

"Didn't you say Ian's mom was going to help out, too?" Stephanie pulled the lid off a plastic container full of fresh-baked cookies.

"I'm sure she's on her way. Ian took Colin to pick up a rental car after church."

"It was nice of her to offer to help out," Emma said.

Lizzie nodded and stood at the sound of a car outside. Through the open window, she could see Cassandra sitting in the car, fussing with her hair in the visor mirror. Lizzie felt her chest tighten. Cassandra was going to be a wonderful mother-in-law, but right now, her presence made Lizzie miss her mom more than ever. When Cassandra stepped out of the car and walked up the driveway, Lizzie moved to the front door and opened it, a warm smile on her face.

"I'm glad you could make it." She stepped back to allow Cassandra to step inside. "You remember Emma, and this is my friend Stephanie."

Emma waved and Stephanie greeted her with a smile. "Nice to meet you, Mrs. Cavanaugh."

"Please, call me Cassie." She set her purse on the couch and took the seat at the end of the table.

"Would you like something to drink?" Lizzie stepped toward the kitchen.

"I'm fine right now, thanks."

Lizzie returned to her place at the table. "We were just getting started."

"I can't wait to see everything you have planned. Ian's tried to keep me updated, but you know how vague men can be when it comes to things like this."

"He's been more involved than most of the groom's I've dealt with at the hotel, but you're right. He couldn't tell the difference between a peony and a David Austin rose."

"I was surprised you didn't choose more tropical colors," Cassandra said.

"I'm not much of a beach person and I love the coziness of the north in the winter. That's one of the reasons I considered having the ceremony in Connecticut. I wanted to bring in some of the cold-weather elements to the wedding."

"She's done an amazing job tying things together in a rustic, yet elegant way," Stephanie said.

"What are you using for the place cards? Ian said something about pine cones."

Lizzie chuckled. "That would be the one thing he'd remember. He was worried about the pine cones having bugs."

Stephanie hopped out of her chair and hurried down the hall. She returned with a pinecone and a purple Christmas ornament. "We sprayed the silver glitter on the pine cones last weekend."

"I thought we could alternate the two as place card holders." Lizzie bit her lip, waiting for Cassandra to respond.

"That will be adorable," Cassandra agreed.

Lizzie relaxed and reached for a box she'd set on the table earlier. "Now, we need to put names on all these cards."

She pulled out several smaller boxes filled with pale, champagne-colored cards, two inches by three in size, a scalloped edge along the top. She pushed a box toward each lady around the table, followed by felt-tipped pens.

"I have a portion of the guest list for each of you, so we aren't duplicating efforts."

Stephanie pulled out a handful of cards. "Where did you land on the final guest count?"

"I have a feeling Jeffrey won't be bringing a guest since he hasn't given me a name yet, so that leaves us at ninety-nine."

Cassandra worried at a butterfly charm on her necklace. "Do you have Dave and Jeffrey seated at the same table?"

"They're both at the head table with the rest of the wedding party."

Cassandra frowned. "Does Dave know Jeffrey is Ian's best man?"

Lizzie's shoulders tensed. "I assume Ian told him. Why? Is there a problem?"

Cassandra's hand stopped moving, but continued to grip the charm. "I'm sure it's fine."

"Cassie, is there something I should know? Ian mentioned replacing Dave over Thanksgiving, too."

"I don't know the whole story." Cassandra dropped her hand to the table. "I'm sure Ian's considered everything, though."

Emma reached over and touched Lizzie's hand. "Why don't you give Ian a call and we'll get started?"

Lizzie pushed several sheets of paper toward Emma, stood and moved down the hall to her bedroom. She shut the door behind her, settled onto the bed, and pressed the speed dial for Ian.

"Miss me already?" he answered with a smile in his voice.

"What's the story between Dave and Jeffrey?"

"What?" Lizzie could hear a door shutting in the background and wondered where he was.

"Your mom seems concerned about Dave and Jeffrey being in the wedding party together. There aren't going to be any problems, are there?"

Ian blew out a loud breath, and Lizzie had to hold the phone away from her ear. "There was an incident between them a few months before Camylle died. I've told Dave how Jeffrey has turned his life around and that we have repaired our friendship, but I'm not sure he believes me."

"What happened?" Lizzie pressed.

"You know Camylle was a tennis player, right?"

"Jeffery told me she was a rising star before the cancer."

"She was. Her coach thought she was ready to go pro. Dave was in town to see me and I took him to one of her matches. Camylle won her first two sets and came out of the locker room during a break, to see Jeffrey.

We were all hanging out, talking, when Dave made some crack about how close the last set had been and she'd been lucky to pull it out. I don't think he meant it the way it came out, but Jeffrey jumped to Camylle's defense. They'd each had a couple of beers, it was hot out, and fists started flying. Camylle tried to break up the fight, but Dave punched her in the face."

Lizzie winced, trying to imagine the mayhem Ian was describing.

"I jumped in and pulled Dave off Jeffrey, holding them apart long enough for Jeffrey to see what had happened. He rushed to her side and took her back to the locker room. After I made sure she was okay, I took Dave back to my place and he left the next day."

Lizzie leaned back on her pillows. "I can see why Jeffrey might not want to see Dave, but your mom made it sound like Dave isn't going to be happy that Jeffrey's your best man. You told him that when you asked him to be a groomsman, right?"

"Not exactly. There's more to the story."

"Of course there is."

"Dave didn't know Camylle well, but they'd met several times when he'd come to visit over the years. When she died, he came to the funeral, more as moral support for me than anything else. Camylle had been my best friend and losing her killed me, despite what Jeffrey thought. I put on a brave face, mostly for him. Now I understand it was the wrong tactic to take with him. I thought he needed my strength to get through the funeral."

Lizzie ran a hand through her hair. "He needed strength but not from you."

"I know. I even knew then that God was the only one who could bring Jeffrey through that pain, but there was no talking to him about that. You saw how he reacted at the mention of God even years after her death."

"What happened at the funeral?"

"I doubt Jeffrey would've known Dave was there, but at the graveside, I started to lose it. Dave stepped up and placed a hand on my shoulder. In doing so, he must have bumped Jeffrey. When Jeffrey turned and saw Dave next to me, I could see pure hatred in Jeffrey's eyes."

"Why?" Lizzie struggled to understand what could make Jeffrey react so violently.

"Jeffrey always had a short temper, but after Camylle was diagnosed, it grew worse. She was the only one he didn't blow up at over every little thing. I pulled Dave back from the grave, but Jeffrey lunged after us. I sent Dave to the car. I had to stop Jeffrey from making a scene."

Lizzie could hear the pain in Ian's words and wished she were with him to take him in her arms.

"When I got to the car, Dave was seething, feeling like I'd sided with Jeffrey. After he went back to Connecticut I didn't hear from him for six months."

"I can't believe neither of you ever told me about this."

Ian sighed. "It wasn't a good time for anyone. Jeffrey kept pushing me away and the one other friend I was comfortable talking with about my grief wasn't speaking to me."

"Have Dave and Jeffrey seen each other since the funeral?"

"There wasn't any reason for them to. By the time Dave called me again, Jeffrey and I were estranged. If I hadn't agreed to talk to you about repairing your floors, we still would be."

"I'm guessing Jeffrey doesn't know Dave is part of the wedding, then, right?"

"I've been meaning to talk to him, but there's been so much going on."

"Ian, you have to tell both of them, today."

"I'll call Jeffrey and see if he's free this evening."

"And Dave?"

"I'll call him too, after I've talked to Jeffrey."

"I'll be praying for you."

"I'm going to need it."

"Call me later."

"I will, and I'm sorry if this is stressing you out. I should have told you before."

"I'll think of a way for you to make it up to me." Lizzie's lips twitched as ideas whirled through her mind.

CHAPTER THIRTY-FIVE

Lizzie returned to the living room where Emma, Stephanie, and Cassandra were chatting and giggling.

"It doesn't sound like much work is getting done in here," Lizzie said as she passed the table on her way to the refrigerator. "Anyone ready for a drink? I have iced tea, soda, water, or I can make some coffee."

With a unanimous response of iced tea, Lizzie pulled out a tall glass pitcher that she set on the counter while she retrieved glasses from the cabinet. Emma arrived at her side to offer assistance and gave Lizzie an encouraging nudge.

"Everything okay?" Emma whispered.

"We'll see." Lizzie carried the pitcher and glasses on a small tray to the table. "Let me see what you've done so far."

Stephanie and Cassandra each held up three cards, the workmanship ranging from comical to downright awful.

"Are you sure you don't want to have these printed? There's a copy shop right around the corner from my house," Stephanie said.

"Wouldn't I have to provide them with a document template or something?"

"They appear to be standard business card size. I have a template I could use, all I'd need is your guest list and seating assignment and I could whip up the document in ten or fifteen minutes."

Lizzie focused on pouring the tea and setting the glasses on napkins Emma had placed on the table. "That still sounds like a lot of work."

"It's not, I promise. Let me do this for you."

Lizzie returned to the kitchen and set the pitcher down. "If you're sure it's that easy."

"Great. I'll go home and put together some samples with different fonts and email them to you. As soon as you choose one I will enter all the names and upload the file to the copy shop. I can even drop off the cards on my way home," she paused to check her watch, "if they're still open. Otherwise I can drop them off in the morning and they should be ready by the time I get home from work."

"And you're sure they'll look nice?"

"I've used them a few times for work projects when our printers have been down or if I didn't want to tie the printers up with a big job. They have samples of some of their work on display, too, and it's pretty impressive."

"All right, I trust your judgment. I don't want to use a very fancy script, maybe something understated."

"I have a few ideas. Give me an hour and then check your email." Stephanie stuffed the card boxes into the larger box, scooped her purse off the floor, and leaned in to give Lizzie a hug before darting out the front door.

"She's a bundle of energy." Cassandra chuckled.

"I've never seen her that excited," Lizzie said, dropping into a chair.

"She mentioned she's been helping out with weddings at her hotel lately. She seemed to light up when she talked about it." Emma twirled one of the handwritten cards.

"Did you get things worked out with Ian?" Cassandra's gaze didn't quite meet Lizzie's.

"He told me about the history between the guys, but neither one of them knows the other is involved in the wedding. He promised to call them both tonight."

"Ian told us about all of the changes he's seen in Jeffrey this past year. I'm sure he and Dave will be able to work things out."

Lizzie tugged on a lock of hair, twirled it around her finger then unwound it again. Her stomach knotted at the idea of an argument between Jeffrey and Dave on her wedding day. Did every relationship in her life have to be complicated?

"Cassandra was telling me she and Colin are looking for some things to do while they are in town." Emma's voice broke through Lizzie's thoughts.

"Hmm?" Lizzie turned to her friend. "Oh yes, I was telling them about all the non-touristy things we have to offer here. I don't do enough of them myself."

"Does Colin play golf?" Emma said, turning to Cassandra.

"Oh yes, he loves it. I don't understand the attraction, but it does keep him out of the house for a few hours when I need to get things done."

"I'll have Ron call him to set up a tee-time, then you and I can hit some of the great boutiques."

"Lizzie was telling us about the shops in Winter Park. I'd love to visit the pet boutique; what was it called?"

"Barky Designs," Lizzie supplied, reaching for another lock of hair.

"That's right. I'm sure I can find a gift to take back for our house sitter. She has a little Yorkie she's always dressing up."

"Lizzie, are you feeling all right?" Emma touched Lizzie's face with the back of her hand.

"A little tired. What were you saying?"

"We were just talking about shopping. Why don't Cassandra and I get out of here and let you get some rest?" Emma stood and collected the empty glasses and soggy napkins, carrying them to the kitchen.

Cassandra pushed back her chair but didn't stand. Instead, she leaned in and reached for Lizzie's hand. "Don't worry about Dave and Jeffrey. They're grown men and I'm sure they can remember this is about you and Ian, not them." She gave Lizzie's hand a squeeze, then stood to go.

Lizzie nodded. "I'm sorry to be such a downer tonight. I know you were looking forward to helping with the place cards."

"I'll do anything you need me to. I just want to be a part of this with you."

Lizzie felt tears stinging her eyes. "I'll see you tomorrow."

CHAPTER THIRTY-SIX

Stephen leaned against the doorframe, watching Lizzie type on her computer. From across the room, he could see dark circles under her eyes. She hadn't said more than good morning to him since she'd arrived an hour before. That made what he needed to do even harder. He reached around the edge of the door and knocked on the wall.

"Got a minute?" he asked when she looked up. He saw her shoulders sag the slightest bit before straightening.

"Sure, come in." She turned her chair away from the computer, giving him her full attention.

"I've been thinking about Mr. Kingsley's job offer." That made her sit up even straighter, maybe even raised her out of her seat a bit. He felt a lump rising in his throat. "Relax, I'm not leaving you in the lurch, but I do want to take the HR position."

Lizzie slumped back in her chair. "It's a great opportunity for you. I think it could be a stepping-stone to even bigger things. You made quite an impression on Mr. Kingsley."

"I wanted to tell you now so you could decide if you wanted to hire another assistant manager or just another concierge. I'll stay until someone else is hired, even give them any training you need me to."

"I appreciate that you have stayed with me this long. I couldn't have made it through this summer and fall without you. I know the uncertainty has been hard on you, especially lately with other people questioning why changes aren't being made."

Stephen nodded, thinking of all the people who'd been asking him when a real group manager was going to be hired, why Lizzie wasn't taking the job, why he wasn't moving into Lizzie's position. Everyone else seemed to have it all figured out.

"I never thought I would stay at Hotel Lago more than a couple of months." He paused, smiling at his memories. "Did I tell you Ben checked in Elaine Henderson last week when I was sick? She didn't even realize he wasn't me."

"Either that is insulting to you or a credit to your training with him. With Elaine, I'm not sure which."

Stephen laughed. "I choose to believe it's a credit to his training. When it's been slow, I've been talking with Ben and Jessica about the personality traits to look for in guests to better tailor service for them, trying to show them how much more this job can be, like you did for me."

"I'm going to miss you around here."

"No you won't. You'll be too busy as the new groups manager." He winked at her.

"What are you talking about? I haven't told anyone I would take that job." Lizzie sat forward and rolled a pen back and forth on the desk.

"Maybe not officially, but I see how much you enjoy it, even when you have to deal with Melvin. You've achieved all you can in this role; it's time to take the next step. Plus, think how happy you will make Chef. I bet he'd make you special lunches for a year."

"We can't both leave. Who will run this place? Jonathan?"

"Well, he did before he let you take the reins. He still oversees the regular front desk operation. Anyway, I hear there's someone from Ryland's corporate office in New York looking to move to Florida."

"Where did you hear that?"

Stephen gave her a playful shrug.

"Why would someone from corporate want to take a job as a concierge manager?"

"A chance to leave cold winters behind and bask in the sun? Part of the agreement Mr. Kingsley made when he bought out Ryland was to give the corporate employees a year to decide if they wanted to move to any opening in our corporate offices or if they wanted to move on. That year will be up in a few more months."

"Is that why you are talking about the HR job now? Are you worried someone from Ryland will snag it from you?"

"No, Mr. Kingsley told me not to worry about that. He's more aware of all you've done for this resort than you know, and understands why I've stayed so long."

"Have you talked to him about your decision?"

"Not yet. I wanted to tell you first."

Lizzie pushed back her chair and came around the desk. Stephen stood as well. "You're not the fresh-faced kid who's afraid of anyone who yells anymore. I'm very proud of you."

She stepped closer and wrapped her arms around him. Her words filled his ears and burned into his brain. They made him feel like a valedictorian at college graduation. He didn't think he'd felt this good at his actual graduation ceremony. Then he'd been full of bravado while secretly terrified about his future. He wanted to memorize every detail of this moment.

When she stepped back, he noticed her rubbing at her eyes. He reached around her for a box of tissues on her desk. When he handed them to her, she laughed.

"I feel like I've turned into a weeping willow."

"You're a bride-to-be; you're allowed to be emotional. Speaking of which, I met the in-laws last night. They seem nice."

Lizzie leaned back against the desk and crossed her ankles. "They are very sweet."

"But?"

"Nothing. I've heard plenty of crazy in-law stories and I know I lucked out with them."

"But?" Stephen persisted.

Lizzie shook her head. "Why do you keep saying that?"

"Because I know you. There's something bothering you and somehow Ian's parents are involved."

"Maybe I trained you too well." She pushed off the desk and returned to her chair.

"So tell me what's wrong." He sat down and removed his glasses, pulling a cloth from his pocket to polish them.

"Nothing's wrong. It's just hard to be around them right now."

He stopped polishing, understanding dawning. He'd learned of the death of her parents the previous year. When everyone was making plans for Thanksgiving and Christmas, he'd been surprised when Lizzie had volunteered to work both holidays. At the last Concierge Club dinner of the year, she'd had an extra glass of wine at dinner and he'd taken her for a cup of coffee after everyone else went home. While they'd sat together over coffee and a shared piece of lemon pound cake, she'd told him about the car accident that had killed both of her parents six years before.

"Because your parents aren't here," he whispered. He put his glasses back on and returned the cloth to his pocket.

Her head dropped to her chest then she lifted her chin and sat up straight. Her armor was back on. "I know they are with me in spirit."

Stephen nodded. "I know we can never replace them, but you have a family of friends who love you very much."

Her lips trembled for a second, then she smiled. "I know, and I am grateful for that. I guess I never thought about getting married after they died. I'm blessed to have Ron and Emma in my life."

She reached for a file folder in a basket on the corner of her desk. Stephen knew the gesture was to end the conversation, but he felt like there was something he needed to say to her.

"Lizzie, I know you have a strong faith in God and that has given you more strength than anyone I've ever known, but you don't always have to lock away your feelings. I think God has put some special people in your life and I like to think I'm one them. You can count on me any time." He stood, gave her a slight nod and left her alone to think about it.

CHAPTER THIRTY-SEVEN

"You don't look so good."

"Good morning to you too, Sheila." Ian passed his assistant's desk and dropped his computer bag on the couch inside his office.

He massaged his neck, trying to loosen the knots from his restless night. Between learning his mother didn't have a venue booked for the rehearsal dinner and having to face the concerns of Jeffrey and Dave being together again, he hadn't slept much. He turned, intending to get a cup of coffee from the kitchen, but Sheila was blocking the doorway.

"Are you feeling all right?" She studied him and he tried to smile.

"I need coffee."

She stepped aside, but followed him to the small kitchen. He could feel her watching his every movement, trying to diagnose his condition based on her years of experience as a mother. He stirred in cream and sugar and took a long sip before turning to face her.

"I had no idea planning a wedding could be so hard on the groom."

Sheila's features relaxed. "It's only hard on a groom who participates in the planning. I thought everything was settled."

"Me too, until I discovered my parents haven't done anything about the rehearsal dinner. It's not like my mother to leave something like this to the last minute."

"That is a bit of a wrinkle, but I'm sure she can figure something out now that she's here."

Ian nodded. "I hope so, because if there's no dinner *and* I have to replace one of my groomsmen, Lizzie might freak out."

"Why would you need to replace a groomsman?"

"There's some bad blood that I took for granted both men had put in the past."

"That sounds more serious than the dinner. You want to talk about it?"

"Thanks, but I think I'm all talked out. I wouldn't mind if you prayed for me and the whole situation."

"Of course." Sheila patted Ian on the shoulder and left him to finish his coffee.

Ian took a seat at the bistro-style table and set his coffee down. In his mind, he replayed his phone call with Jeffrey the previous evening. He should have known the moment Jeffrey answered the call that it wasn't the right time to tell him about Dave being in the wedding. Jeffrey sounded edgy and distracted, but the moment Dave's name was mentioned his attention focused.

"I didn't even know you were still friends with him," Jeffrey had grumbled.

"Dave and I were friends long before I met you. If you remember, I hadn't seen you in almost four years before Lizzie brought us back into each other's lives."

"Why'd she have to bring her cookies to *my* construction site?"

Jeffrey's begrudging tone had surprised Ian. "Let's keep her out of this, please. It's between you, me, and Dave."

"I can't believe he agreed when you told him I was your best man."

"Well..."

This had brought an angry laugh from Jeffrey. "You didn't tell him, did you? Does he even know we're friends again?"

"Yes, and I've told him about the changes in your life. He's understandably skeptical."

"Thanks for the heads up. If you don't mind, I need to go." Without waiting for an answer, Jeffrey had hung up.

Ian shook his head and lifted his now tepid cup of coffee to his mouth. He rose, dumped the remaining liquid and rinsed the cup in the sink before wandering back to his office. He paused in the doorway and glanced back at Sheila.

"Would you mind calling Arnaldo to see if he has any openings for the sixteenth? I think we will have around twenty in the party."

"I'll check and let you know. Do you want me to look for any other places in case he is full?"

"If anything comes to mind, jot it down and I'll give the information to my mom."

Sheila nodded and reached for the phone. Ian stepped inside his office and closed the door, hoping the quiet would help him focus on work. In the spring, he'd uploaded some home designs he'd created to his website. He wasn't sure there was a market for them in a town that seemed obsessed with cookie-cutter neighborhoods, but Sheila had encouraged him after seeing the sketches.

When requests started coming in, not only for the designs online, but for custom home plans as well, he'd been pleasantly surprised. His calendar all summer and fall had been filled with creating new plans, even working with interior and landscape designers to put together dream homes. It took more clients to make the same money as a corporate account, but he enjoyed the work much more.

He straddled the stool at his drafting table and flipped back the protective cover page to reveal his current project. The client was a man who'd made his fortune in the steel industry and was now building his retirement home. Ian couldn't imagine how the widower would use twenty thousand square feet of living space. It seemed obscene for a single person, but it had been fun designing it. Ian had even partnered with the local college for arts and design to build the most advanced home theater in the state.

"Mr. Cavanaugh?" Sheila's voice came through the intercom.

Ian slipped off the stool and moved to his desk. "Yes, Sheila."

"Arnaldo is booked until nine-thirty on the sixteenth. He said he could hold the rest of the night for you if that would work."

"Thanks. Do you think he would mind holding onto that space for a day? I don't know how long the rehearsal will be."

"It's already done."

"What would I do without you?"

"Lose all your clients and go bankrupt, I'm sure."

Ian chuckled. "I'll call my mom and let her know."

"Don't forget, Mr. Winston is coming in at eleven to review the final plans."

"I'm looking at them right now. Let me know when he arrives." Ian clicked off the intercom and glanced back at the drafting table. There wasn't anything left to do on the sketch, unless Mr. Winston asked for more changes. Feeling confident he had plenty of time before the meeting, Ian sat down and dialed the number for Hotel Lago.

CHAPTER THIRTY-EIGHT

Cassandra slipped on the plush hotel bathrobe and padded to one of the large windows overlooking Lake Eola. A pair of swans followed by three cygnets, cut through the water with ease, leaving the tiniest wake behind them.

"Can you believe this?" she called over her shoulder to her husband.

"Believe what?"

"It's sunny and warm in December. I bet it's overcast and in the forties at home." She turned away from the window in time to see Colin stepping out of the bathroom. He wore a towel around his waist and used another to dry his thick black hair. Even at sixty-one he was still a fine looking man. She crossed the room and took the towel from his hand.

"I wasn't finished," Colin said.

Cassandra reached up and caressed his face. "Can you believe our baby is getting married?"

Colin leaned down and kissed her, brushing a lock of hair off her forehead as he pulled back. "He hasn't been a baby for a long time now."

"You know what I mean." She swatted at him.

He stepped to the window and looked out over the park. "It is beautiful here. I can see why Ian didn't want to leave the state after college. I imagine after four winters like these he wouldn't ever want to return to the frigid north."

Cassandra moved beside him and rested her head on his arm. "We'll be so far away from our grandbabies."

Colin laughed. "Don't rush things. Let's get through the wedding first. Speaking of which, do you have any ideas for the rehearsal dinner?"

She shook her head. "As many parties as I have planned, I feel completely unprepared for this."

Colin slipped his arm around Cassandra and she nestled her head on his chest. "You know we aren't losing Ian, right? If anything, we're gaining the daughter you always wanted."

She sighed. "Only if she wants us."

"Lizzie hasn't done anything to indicate she doesn't want us. I saw how happy she was on the video conference. She was excited to share that moment with us."

"You're right. I'm being overly sensitive."

The telephone rang in the sitting room. Cassandra moved out of her husband's arms and passed through the arched doorway and reached for the phone. "Hello?"

"Good morning, mom."

"Ian, shouldn't you be at work?"

"I am but I have a few minutes before my client arrives. Sheila called Arnaldo and he has space for the rehearsal dinner at nine thirty. I told her it would be about twenty guests."

"Twenty? Does that sound right?" Cassandra ran through the wedding party in her head. "I was thinking closer to fifteen."

"I don't know. Maybe you and Sheila should get together this afternoon. She's married off three sons. Let me get her on the line."

"Sure I can help out," Sheila said when Ian conferenced her in. "I can meet you for lunch."

"Sheila, you're an angel. Where and when?"

Cassandra noted the details down, and as she finished the call, Colin entered the sitting room, dressed in a pair of khaki pants and a turquoise polo. "Who was that?"

"Ian and his assistant, Sheila. I'm meeting her for lunch and she's going to help me plan this dinner. I forgot she has three sons who are all married. I should have called her months ago."

"I'm sure she will get you squared away in no time. Ian was fortunate to find her. She's as reliable as a Swiss watch." Colin slipped on a pair of shoes. "I'm going to grab some breakfast in the lounge. Would you like me to bring you anything?"

"A cup of coffee and a bagel would be nice."

"Will do. Back in ten minutes or so."

"Take your time."

When Colin left, Cassandra went to the window again. Two children were chasing each other in the park. She could imagine their joyful laughter. How could anyone be less than joyful in such a setting? Turning her back on the window, she moved to the closet and picked out an outfit before going into the bathroom to get dressed.

Ten minutes later, she emerged feeling calmer than she had in weeks. Knowing she had Sheila helping her now had relieved most of her anxiety. The room door opened and Colin entered carrying a tray, which he sat on a small dining room table in an alcove by the window.

"Stephen insisted I bring you some fresh fruit along with the bagel. I can see why Lizzie is so proud of him. He knows the preferences of everyone in that lounge."

"How is that possible?"

"Well, there were only three other people when I was in there," Colin admitted with a grin, "and apparently they are regulars."

"That's still impressive. I can't even remember if it's you or Ian who likes cantaloupe."

Colin scrunched his nose in disgust. "That would be Ian."

"Have you talked to Ron about golfing yet?"

"No, are we supposed to?"

"Last night Emma said she was going to have him call you."

"I'm sure he'll call sometime today."

Cassandra couldn't help laughing when the phone started ringing. "I bet it's for you."

Colin answered it and winked at her. "Yes, Ron, we were just talking about you."

CHAPTER THIRTY-NINE

Cheers and laughter floated down the hallway as Jeffrey approached the men's Bible study room. A dozen guys surrounded a ping-pong table where a match between Paul and Chad was in progress. A couple of the guys waved at Jeffrey as he entered before returning their attention to the game. Five minutes later, the final game point was won and Chad was named the victor.

"Good game," Paul said, extending his hand to his opponent.

Chad grinned. "Looking forward to my free lunch Sunday."

The men dispersed and began taking seats at the other end of the room. Jeffrey found an empty chair at the end of a row near the back. Paul sat down next to him.

"How did things go with Michelle? You've been on my mind all week. I thought about calling when I didn't hear from you, but I didn't want to push."

"Sorry about that. I guess I'm not used to having other people interested in my life."

Paul nodded. "You want to get a coffee after we finish here?"

"Yeah, that would be good."

"All right, everyone," Chad announced, "now we have established I am the king of the ping pong table, why don't we get started with our study." There were ripples of laughter before he quieted them for the opening prayer.

"I meant to give this to you Sunday," Paul whispered, handing Jeffrey a book.

Jeffrey recognized it as the study guide all the other men were now opening. "Thanks."

"Last week we completed chapter one, looking at Paul's background. I hope everyone had a chance to read through chapter two, Paul's conversion experience. Have any of you participated in an intervention for a friend or family member?"

A few raised their hands. "We do interventions to try to change the path someone is on. We usually think of struggles with addiction, but wallowing in grief or bitterness also keeps us from living healthy lives.

"Paul wasn't involved in any of these things. He was an upstanding Jew, *his* vice was not believing in the resurrected Messiah, and God conducted a supernatural intervention to get Paul on the correct path."

Jeffrey didn't bother opening the book, but sat back and listened to Chad's words on the difference between the moment of conversion and the act of baptism. Jeffrey didn't understand the point of baptism and hadn't taken part in it himself.

"Would anyone like to share the story of how your life has changed since you entered a relationship with Christ?" Chad looked out over the group.

There was quiet for almost a minute before a man on the other side of the room stood and spoke. Jeffrey listened to the man's story, blown away at how open and honest he was being with the group. Several others shared as well before Chad asked another question.

"Some of you covered this in your testimonies, but would anyone like to share how they resisted the message of salvation?"

A lance shot through Jeffrey's heart. He knew how guilty he was of resisting the message. He hadn't listened when the woman he loved shared her faith with him. Bitterness had filled him when her faith hadn't faltered after her cancer diagnosis, nor at any point in her rapid decline. He wasn't even sure why, four years later, his heart had softened when Lizzie shared with him her own struggles with faith.

"That's all for tonight. I hope this provides you with encouragement for the rest of the week." Chairs creaked as the men stood and filed out of the rows.

"You okay?" Paul asked.

"Yeah, just thinking."

"Ready to get that coffee?"

Jeffrey nodded and stood. Paul stopped to talk with a couple of guys and Jeffrey followed, still lost in thought.

"Same place, five minutes?" Paul pulled a set of keys out his pants' pocket as the men started down the stairs to the main floor.

"Sure." Jeffrey found his truck and climbed inside. He saw Paul backing a black Accord out of a spot a couple of rows over and followed him out of the parking lot.

"You sure you're all right?" Paul asked after they'd arrived and were sitting down with their drinks. "You seem kind of dazed."

Jeffrey ran a hand along his jaw and exhaled. "A lot on my mind."

"That's why we are here, to talk it out. Tell me what happened with Michelle."

Jeffrey recapped his conversation with her. "I didn't know how to translate her intellectual knowledge to a heartfelt belief. I'm still trying to understand a lot of the intellectual stuff myself."

"Sometimes people analyze things so much all they can see is facts, but it sounds like she may be starting to open up her heart. You did the right thing by encouraging her to call Wendy. If she's holding onto bitterness and regret from her past relationships, it may be easier for her to speak to another woman about those feelings."

"I admit, telling her to call Wendy feels like a way to extricate myself from the situation. I was in over my head."

"You did fine. Remember, when we are put in a position to share with someone the gift of God's love and redemption, we aren't alone. We only need to open up our hearts to hear the words He wants us to say."

"I think I'm still a long way from hearing God speak to me." Jeffrey ran his thumbnail over the lip of the cup lid making a tink-tink-tink noise.

"If you keep thinking that way, then yes you are, but if you are studying the Bible and opening a dialogue with Him through prayer, you have just as much access to hearing His words as I do. You've been a believer for a year now, right?" Jeffrey nodded and Paul continued. "Just like you had to learn to walk and learn to talk as an infant, you have to learn how to walk in Christ. You do that by studying His word and getting involved in group fellowship."

"Lizzie and Ian have been telling me I need to get more involved, but I didn't understand why until last weekend. When you offered to have the guys pray for me during my meeting with Michelle," Jeffrey looked down at his cup, "it gave me strength."

Paul smiled. "That's what it's all about, members of the body strengthening each other."

CHAPTER FORTY

With his cell phone in one hand, more than an inch from his ear, Ian rested his forehead in his other hand. He didn't know how much longer he could listen to Dave's angry tirade. After playing phone tag for three days, Ian had finally connected with his old friend. Dave's reaction to learning Jeffrey was going to be the best man in the wedding had been far harsher than expected.

When the yelling stopped, Ian waited another thirty seconds before speaking. "Dave, I'm sorry I didn't tell you to begin with. Wait," Ian said as Dave started shouting again. "Listen, I understand if you don't want to be in the wedding anymore. I can ask someone else, but I hope you will still be there. I really want you there."

"I didn't say I wouldn't be in the wedding. I just think you're making a big mistake having that arrogant snot as your best man. I wouldn't be surprised if he found himself too busy or too drunk to show up."

"I told you, he's changed. He hasn't had a drink, well, he had a slip in February, but since then not a drop. If it hadn't been for Jeffrey I wouldn't have met Lizzie. We've settled our differences and I know I can depend on him."

Dave only grunted.

"If you still want to be in the wedding, I need you to promise you won't cause any scenes with Jeffrey. I can't allow our past to ruin Lizzie's big day."

"It's your big day too," Dave countered.

"As long as she is happy I will be happy. She had to overcome a lot more to get to this point than I did."

"I can't wait to meet her. I wish I could come in earlier, but..."

"Don't worry about it. I know Lizzie is going to be pushing herself to make sure everything at the hotel is buttoned up before we leave for the honeymoon. I'll be lucky to drag her out in time for the rehearsal."

"Where are you going for your honeymoon?"

"I'm not at liberty to say." Ian grinned. He was impressed with himself for managing to keep this secret.

"Come on, who am I going to tell?"

"This is the one part of the wedding Lizzie has left completely in my hands and I want it to be a surprise. I'm not taking any chances of someone leaking information. She has a way of making people talk." Ian thought back on those first weeks when she'd seemed to open up both Jeffrey and Ian. It wasn't anything she said or did, but the way she listened that made people want to tell her everything.

"All right, I hope it's someplace nice and not Vegas."

"Give me some credit. I have more taste than that. What time does your flight get in again?"

"Seven forty-five Wednesday night."

"I'll be there to pick you up."

"You don't have to do that. I can catch a cab."

"No way. The drive will give us time to catch up."

Ian hung up the phone, still worried about how Dave and Jeffery would react when they saw each other the following week. Dave had been a lot more vocal than Jeffrey, which led Ian to fear Jeffrey's anger might be simmering, waiting for the wrong moment to boil over.

"Lord, only you can keep these guys from erupting at the wedding. Please soften their hearts and help them to forgive each other."

An alarm trilled on his cell phone and he silenced it as he grabbed his keys and headed out the front door.

CHAPTER FORTY-ONE

"I Heard the Bells on Christmas Day" by Mercy Me played on the radio, accompanied by the hum of the old Camry's tires as Lizzie navigated along Orange Avenue. When her alarm had gone off at eight, she'd hit the snooze button three times. She would have stayed in bed longer if she hadn't had the dress fitting at ten. She worried she may have lost even more weight in the past week.

"Thank you for letting me come along." Cassandra's voice penetrated Lizzie's thoughts as she pulled into a parking space.

She nodded but couldn't bring herself to speak. Up to this point, Mona and Stephanie were the only ones who had seen Lizzie's dress. It had been too painful to include even Emma in the shopping process. Now, both of her mother figures would be present at this final fitting.

A large Red Cedar tree in the park across from the train station sparkled with oversized ornaments reflecting the warm sun. With only fifteen days to Christmas, Park Avenue was filled with frenzied shoppers, and Emma's tranquil face stood out in the harried crowd. Lizzie quickened her pace.

Emma leaned in to embrace Lizzie as they met. "It's good to see you, Cassie," she said over Lizzie's shoulder, then together they walked to the bridal boutique.

"Good morning, Ms. Reynolds," the clerk greeted Lizzie the moment she stepped inside. "You must be the mother of the bride." The clerk extended her hand to Cassandra.

"Actually, I'm Cassandra, the groom's mother."

Lizzie noticed the flush in Cassandra's cheeks and felt her own grow warm. "My mom died a few years ago."

The clerk's discomfort was immediate. Lizzie linked her arm through Emma's soft brown one. "And this is Emma. She's become a surrogate mother to me."

"It's a pleasure meeting you both." The clerk regained her professional demeanor and led them to the dressing area. "Why don't you two ladies have a seat while I help Ms. Reynolds with her dress."

Lizzie followed the clerk into a dressing room and changed into it. She could tell right away that the dress was even looser than the previous week. When the clerk stepped back to appraise her, Lizzie could see the look of concern in the other woman's eyes.

"You've lost more weight."

"It's been a difficult week." Lizzie studied her reflection in the mirror but it felt like a stranger looked back at her. Her eyes were tired and red, her skin pale and lackluster. The dress was still a wondrous creation, but it didn't fall quite right along her curves. "How am I supposed to get married looking like this?"

The clerk stepped forward and placed her hands on Lizzie's shoulders. "Everything will be fine. I told my seamstress to come in this morning just in case this happened. I'll go get her."

Lizzie leaned against the wall, turning her back on the mirror. A whisper of fear passed through her. Was this a sign she should postpone the wedding?

"Lord, I know these fears are unfounded. I know Ian is the man you have chosen for me. I know I am worthy of his love. Father, protect me from this attack, guard my heart and mind. Give me Your courage and peace to carry on for one more week." She closed her eyes and took several deep breaths until the fears subsided and her heartbeat slowed to normal.

The dressing room door opened and the clerk entered, followed by a petite Filipino woman. "Ms. Reynolds, this is Mali."

Mali studied Lizzie without speaking, then twirled a finger, indicating Lizzie should turn around. She did so and felt Mali's hands on her waist. The fabric of her dress was pulled and clipped in several places before Mali's hands turned Lizzie to face her again. After another minute of study Mali nodded.

"If you want to show your lady friends, go now, then come back and turn it inside out for me to pin adjustments." Mali stepped back into a corner.

Lizzie looked in the mirror. Whatever Mali had done, the dress seemed more flattering than ever. Taking a deep breath, Lizzie opened the door and stepped out into the salon area. The conversation between Emma and Cassandra stopped mid-sentence when Lizzie approached them. She stepped up onto the small dais and did a slow turn for them. When she faced them again, she saw tears streaming down their faces and blinked to control her own.

"You look so beautiful," Emma breathed. Cassandra nodded in agreement as she reached into her purse and retrieved a pack of tissues. She handed one to Emma and they each wiped their faces.

"You're going to take Ian's breath away," Cassandra said.

"Mali needs to make some adjustments. I'll be another ten or fifteen minutes. Do you want to shop a little before lunch?" Lizzie was surprised at the calmness of her words when she felt like her heart was being squeezed.

"Text me when you are finished and we can meet back up." Emma stood but Cassandra remained seated, her gaze never leaving Lizzie. "Come on, Cassie. I think we missed a couple of stores the other day."

Lizzie retreated to the dressing room and submitted to the clerk's helping hands, removing the dress, turning it inside out and putting it on again. Mali stepped out of the corner and began working. Lizzie closed her eyes and followed the directions she was given, holding back the tears. She may have never dreamed of a wedding as a little girl, but the past eight months she'd done nothing but dream about sharing this moment with her mother.

"All done, Ms. Reynolds. I have this ready for you Monday." Mail gathered the dress and slipped out of the dressing room. Lizzie changed back into her clothes and sat there for several minutes until there was a quiet knock on the door. The clerk poked her head inside.

"I thought you might like a glass of water." The clerk extended a tall, slender glass.

Lizzie accepted it and allowed the cool liquid to roll down her throat. She didn't know if she could face having lunch with Emma and Cassandra. Emma could always take Cassandra back to the hotel.

"I don't see many mother-in-laws in here," the clerk said, "but I can tell Cassandra loves you very much. You're a lucky woman."

Lizzie nodded. "Cassie has been good to me and I do love her dearly. God must have known it would take two women to replace my mom."

"He didn't replace her, He just made a substitution."

The clerk's words zoomed right into Lizzie's heart and she smiled, feeling a dark cloud lifting from her. "You're so right. Thank you, for everything. You've been kind and patient through this whole process. I can't believe it will all be over in a week."

The clerk took the empty glass. "It's been a pleasure working with you. Why don't you stop by Monday night and we'll give the dress one more test, make sure Mali didn't get over zealous on those tucks? Does six thirty sound good?"

"Perfect." Lizzie gathered her purse and the bag she'd brought her shoes in. "I'll see you then."

CHAPTER FORTY-TWO

Michelle stepped outside to a crystal clear Sunday morning. The entire week had brought beautiful weather that anyone north of the Mason-Dixon line would have envied, but it was wasted on Michelle. She'd gone through the hours at work on autopilot and she'd spent her off time reading the Bible. She had started in Genesis an hour after Jeffrey left the previous week and had made it through Matthew. She'd almost quit when she reached Leviticus, but something made her plough on.

The church before her was massive, much larger than the place she normally attended. She hesitated when she reached the rear of her car and contemplated going home, but the same force that had kept her reading the Bible pulled her toward the church doors.

"Michelle? Hey."

She turned to find Wendy approaching her. Two other women were close behind; too late to turn back now.

"Hi, Wendy." Michelle hoped she sounded perkier than she felt.

"I'd like you to meet my friends, Barbara and Lily." Wendy pointed at each lady in turn. "This is Michelle."

"Nice to meet you," Barbara said.

"Is this your first time here?" This came from Lily.

"I usually go to a different church, but I knew Wendy came here. I thought I would check it out." Michelle could feel Wendy's eyes on her, but kept her attention focused on the other two ladies.

"We're glad you came." Lily led the way into the sanctuary. Barbara followed and Wendy linked arms with Michelle.

Michelle shook her off. "Are you afraid I'm going to run off? I chose to be here."

"And I'm happy to see you. You just looked like you might need some moral support to get inside. You've been quiet at work, everything okay?"

"I've been doing a lot of thinking."

"Sometimes you have to stop thinking and start feeling." Wendy filed into a pew near the back, behind Barbara and Lily. Michelle was grateful they hadn't gone to the front of the church. This way, if she needed to make a fast escape the whole congregation wouldn't see her.

The choir was taking the stage as the women settled into their seats and soon the first song began. So far nothing different from the church she'd been attending. She wasn't sure why she thought it would be. She followed along, the words projected onto large screens at the front. After fifteen minutes of songs, Michelle was thankful to sit down.

"Welcome, everyone," the pastor greeted the crowd. He was young and energetic, the polar opposite of the old and lethargic minister at her own church. "It's good to see so many people in the Lord's house. Have you all finished your Christmas shopping?"

There were chuckles around the room. "I haven't. I'm one of those men out on Christmas Eve searching for everyone on my list. After our first two Christmases together my wife told me not to worry about getting her anything, she'd just choose a gift for herself. I thought I'd hit the jackpot, the best wife ever, until the first Christmas she chose her own gift.

"You know what she chose? Not a diamond necklace or a fancy perfume. No, she chose a new chainsaw because I'd kept putting off trimming some dead trees in our backyard. I thought that was a fluke until the second year when she chose a five-gallon bucket of paint and an assortment of rollers for me to repaint the house. After that I told her I would be more than happy to search for the perfect gift."

Michelle found herself relaxing, enjoying the story. She glanced around, admiring the festively arranged garlands and wreaths.

"Of course, I can't ever give her any gift better than the one she received fifteen years ago when she accepted Christ as her savior. It can be hard on a guy's ego to know he's always going to be second best, but in this case I can make an exception. I'm thankful Jesus Christ sacrificed himself so my wife and I can spend eternity together. With Christmas only a couple of weeks away, how many of you are taking time to remember that perfect gift that nothing on earth can ever supersede?"

The pastor's words faded away as Michelle's thoughts drifted to everything she'd read over the past year, all of the sermons she'd attended, everything Jeffrey had said and done. It was Jeffrey's actions that stood out the most. His kindness and concern in February when he'd heard of Amanda's death and reached out to her even though they had parted on bad terms months before. His patience with her when she didn't buy into his faith. His understanding when she'd lied to him to avoid her feelings. His acceptance when he'd thought she was dating someone else. His willingness to give her space and understanding when she hadn't been comfortable talking to him. She'd never known anyone so bereft of ulterior motive.

"Jesus' birth may be the most humble event ever recorded. His life was lived modestly. He loved all those he came in contact with, even those he knew would betray him. To his last breath he asked God the Father to forgive them for their sin. We are called to live like Jesus did, but how many of us can say we do? We battle pride, anger, jealousy, and bitterness, resentment, lust, apathy, and more every single day.

"Do our lives reflect God's love as we battle these feelings? Only through the Holy Spirit living within us can we overcome the pull of the world. Are any of you here today living without the Holy Spirit? Have you been resisting the tug of Jesus on your heart? Now is the time to take that final step, to submit to God's will and allow Him to be the Lord of your life."

A piano started playing and Michelle noticed several of the people nearby were bowing their heads. The pastor looked down at the floor for several minutes and Michelle wondered if there had been some cue to start praying that she'd missed.

The pastor looked up again and scanned the crowd. "I feel the presence of God moving in here this morning. Do you feel it too?"

Murmurs of "Amen" rippled around the room. Michelle felt the flesh on her arm prickle into chill bumps, while her hands felt clammy. She wiped them on her pants.

"We're going to sing a song and I'm going to ask the associate pastors to join me up here. If there is anyone here who is ready to answer the call of Christ, I invite you to come forward. We want to pray with you."

The piano changed to the opening prelude of "Amazing Grace". Michelle's mouth felt dry, her heart was racing, and still her skin felt like she was out in a winter storm.

"I once was blind, but now I see." Michelle heard Wendy singing beside her and turned to see her friend had her eyes closed, head tipped up to the sky.

Michelle felt her legs moving, then she was standing. A minute later she was moving past the rows of pews toward the front of the church. She didn't understand where she was going or how she was getting there. Her eyes met those of the pastor and her feet seemed to move faster.

The pastor's eyes were grey and soft, like the fur of a kitten she'd had as a child. As she moved closer, she saw his arm extend and then wrap around her shoulder. He turned his back to the congregation and spoke softly.

"How can we pray for you today?"

"I ... believe," Michelle whispered. "It's ... all ... true."

"Are you ready to accept Jesus as your Lord and Savior?"

Michelle nodded. The pastor squeezed her shoulder.

"Repeat this prayer with me: Lord God in heaven, thank you for sending your son Jesus to die for my sins. I ask for your forgiveness and pray that you will be the ruler of my life. Give me a heart to serve You in all I do."

Michelle repeated the words and felt the magnetic tug that had been controlling her all week relax and settle into a happy thrum inside her chest.

CHAPTER FORTY-THREE

As the congregation filed out of the church, Jeffrey approached Michelle, their eyes locked on each other. He wondered if Lizzie had felt this same enormous sense of relief mixed with pride the night he had given his own life to Christ. Michelle dropped her gaze.

"It's good to see you," Jeffrey said.

Michelle didn't lift her head, but he could see her eyes move, looking at him through the veil of her eyelashes. "So now what?"

Jeffrey's laughter reverberated around the church. He'd given her a pamphlet he'd received from Lizzie after his conversion. The title had been *I'm Saved, Now What?* Michelle had told him she'd read it; he had a sneaking suspicion she'd probably worn it out over the past year.

"I can get you a new copy of the pamphlet if you haven't already memorized the original," he teased.

This brought a smile to her face and at last she met his gaze. "I can't believe I did this, but now I feel … I don't know what the words are."

"I think the word I used was 'freeing'," he paused and grinned, "then I asked Lizzie, 'What now?'."

Michelle pushed him. "Don't make fun of me."

Jeffrey stumbled back a couple of steps. "I'm not. That's what I said and she had me call Ian. I'd tell you to call Wendy, but I'm sure she's still around here somewhere."

He glanced over his shoulder but by now the church was empty. "I'm surprised she wasn't up here with you."

"It's not like I told her what I was doing. I didn't even know myself until the pastor started praying with me."

"Hey, Jeffrey, are you coming to lunch?"

Jeffrey turned to see Paul, poking his head through a door at the back of the church. "Come in here a minute. I'd like you to meet someone."

Paul pulled the door open wider and strode down the long aisle. "You're the girl who accepted Christ this morning. Welcome to the family."

"Paul, this is Michelle. Michelle, this is my friend Paul."

The pair shook hands and Paul shot Jeffrey a questioning glance. "The Michelle?"

Jeffrey nodded.

"What does that mean?" she asked. Her words reminded Jeffrey of an angry cat he'd encountered in an alley one night, hackles raised, legs coiled ready to attack.

"Paul knows Wendy, too," Jeffrey jumped in before Paul could reply.

"Uh-huh," but she didn't sound convinced that was the whole story.

"I thought I'd take Michelle out to lunch to celebrate," Jeffrey said.

"All right, I'll tell the guys. See you Wednesday?"

"I should be there unless Ian calls me with some wedding emergency."

"Oh, right, that's next weekend. Well, if something comes up and we don't see you before, have a great Christmas." Paul gave Jeffrey a bro-hug and slapped him on the back. "Good to meet you, Michelle."

Jeffrey watched the other man retreat, hoping Michelle wouldn't ask questions about how much Paul knew about her. When the door closed, he looked her way again.

"Where are you taking me for lunch?" Michelle started moving up the aisle.

"Wherever you want to go. We can invite Wendy, too, if you want."

Michelle turned into a pew and bent down to collect her purse. "If she's still outside, we can ask, but she may have plans with some of her friends. How does the Cheesecake Factory sound?"

Jeffrey's mouth started watering. "Sounds good."

They stepped outside and a cool breeze ruffled his hair. Several groups of people milled around, enjoying the reprieve from the week's heat. It was hard to believe Christmas was only a little more than two weeks away.

"There she is." Michelle grabbed Jeffrey by the hand and pulled him toward a cluster of women. Wendy peeled off from the group and ran toward them, squealing in delight. She threw her arms around Michelle and must have squeezed too tight because Jeffrey saw Michelle's eyes bulge a little.

"I'm so happy," Wendy said.

"I keep hearing that. It was strange having complete strangers telling me how happy they were for me."

"Well, I'm no stranger and I'm glad your head finally talked your heart into believing. What changed?"

"I don't know." Michelle glanced at Jeffrey. "I heard something that made me look at things from a different perspective."

"Whatever it was, I'm glad you are part of the family now. We were getting ready to go to lunch, do you two want to join us?"

"Um, Jeffrey and I were going to grab something."

Wendy nodded and winked. "I'll see you tomorrow."

When Wendy was out of earshot Jeffrey asked, "What was that wink about?"

Michelle gave a dismissive wave. "That's just Wendy. Your car or mine?"

"I'll drive; the truck's right over there." He pointed and pulled his keys from his pocket. When they reached it, he opened the door for her and made sure she didn't need any help getting in. As he walked around the front, he noticed a piece of paper underneath his windshield wiper. Reaching the driver side, he pulled it out and couldn't keep himself from laughing.

Now you can ask her to the wedding.

He was still laughing when he climbed into the truck.

"What's so funny?"

He handed her the sheet of paper.

"What does it mean? Who wrote that? It's not Wendy's handwriting."

Jeffrey sobered and turned toward her. "It means: I like you and I want you to be my date at Lizzie's wedding, but that doesn't imply I am looking for a serious relationship, not yet anyway. Would you like to go with me?"

Michelle shrugged. "I thought you'd never ask. What time are you picking me up?"

CHAPTER FORTY-FOUR

"I'll see you tomorrow, Sheila." Ian paused at his assistant's desk on his way out of the office.

"I hope everything goes well tonight."

"A few extra prayers wouldn't hurt. Dave hasn't said much about seeing Jeffrey tonight."

"I will be praying for you. Try to have fun." She stood and gave him a hug before he left.

Outside, the sky was pale purple, the sun already beyond the western horizon. A brisk wind rustled the bare sycamore trees around the property. Ian slipped into his BMW and let the engine run for a minute while he dialed Dave's cell phone number.

"Hey, I'm leaving work now. I should be at your hotel in ten minutes."

"Sounds good. I'll meet you out front."

Hanging up, Ian pulled out of the parking lot and used side streets to avoid the rush hour traffic. Dave was outside when Ian pulled up to Hotel Lago.

"So, what's the plan tonight?"

"We're meeting a few guys at Houston's for a nice steak dinner."

"Sounds like a wild night. You realize this is your bachelor party, right?"

"You know I'm not a wild guy. We may go see a band. Jeffery was supposed to find out if there's anyone good playing tonight."

"I'm sure he knows all the bar schedules," Dave grumbled.

"I told you he doesn't do that scene anymore. He has a friend in a band, though, and she was going to check with her contacts to see what's going on tonight."

"This doesn't look like a steakhouse," Dave said when Ian parked outside a shopping center.

"We're getting some coffee first. Come on." Ian got out of the car and entered a nondescript shop before Dave could respond.

Inside, Jeffrey sat at a table near the back, a large take-out cup in one hand and half of a Danish in the other. He raised the cup in welcome when Ian entered.

"How'd you find this place?" Jeffrey asked.

"Lizzie told me about it. She found it on one of her dress shopping expeditions and has been coming nearly every weekend since."

"This is the best bear claw I've ever had." Jeffrey devoured the last of the pastry and licked his fingers.

The door opened and Dave stepped inside. Ian saw Dave tense when his gaze landed on Jeffrey. Ian moved toward Dave and steered his friend to the table. Why don't you two talk while I get us some coffee? You need anything else, Jeffrey?"

"I'm good, but you should try the bear claws."

Ian headed off to place an order. Out of the corner of his eye, he watched his two friends. Dave was still standing, stone-faced, while Jeffrey remained seated, sipping on his drink. Neither seemed willing to make the first move.

"Can I help you?" A young woman in a tight black t-shirt and jeans stood behind the counter, ready to take his order.

"Two medium coffees and a bear claw, please."

She rang up the items and gave him a total, which he handed over, his ears still tuned to the back corner. A woman in her mid-thirties, typing on a laptop, oblivious to anyone else, occupied one other table in the cafe.

"Why don't you sit down," he heard Jeffrey say.

"I'm fine standing."

"Suit yourself."

Silence fell again while Ian waited for the coffees. When the cashier handed him the cups and a bag with the pastry, he turned back to the table.

"Do you want cream or sugar, Dave?"

"Nah, black's fine."

Ian stopped at a side table to add cream and sugar to his own and to collect a handful of napkins.

"Here you go," he said, handing a cup to Dave. "Why don't you sit down?"

Dave pulled out a chair and sat, but kept a good foot between himself and the table.

"Look, I'm sorry about the way I acted at Camylle's funeral," Jeffrey said. "I was out of line. I'm not the same guy anymore, though. Can we call a truce for the wedding? This weekend is about Ian and Lizzie."

Ian studied Dave, waiting for the other man to make his own apology.

"Truce, for Ian, but that doesn't mean we're going to be friends."

Jeffrey bowed his head. "That's fine as long as we can be civil with each other through the next couple of days. Lizzie deserves a perfect wedding."

Ian thought he saw Dave's face soften a tiny bit. "You want some of this bear claw?" he offered Dave.

Dave ripped off a piece and popped it into his mouth. "That *is* good," he mumbled around the pastry.

Jeffrey set his cup on the table. "Who else are we meeting for dinner?"

"Stephen and a few guys from church. Did Michelle find any good bands?"

"She told me about a little club in Winter Park. They have jazz and blues bands almost every night. Sounds low key, right up your alley." Jeffrey grinned.

"So I don't want to get drunk and go to a strip club. It's not like I asked to go to a make-your-own pottery studio." Ian was beginning to wonder if the whole evening would be peppered with jibes at his choice of activities.

"Calm down, I'm just messing with you. I couldn't even begin to picture you in a strip club. Heck, I can't see myself there anymore." Jeffrey scratched his chin.

Dave choked and coffee spewed from his nose and dribbled from his mouth.

Jeffrey leveled his gaze at Dave. "What was it, the picture of Ian with a bunch of dancing girls or me not in such a place that got you?"

"Both," Dave said between gasps. He coughed several more times before taking the napkins Ian offered. He wiped his face and blew his nose, while Ian cleaned up the table.

"To be honest, I only went to a strip club once. The whole time I felt like Camylle was watching me." Jeffrey shrugged. "Now I think she may have been looking down from heaven, and disappointed with what I'd become. There's a lot I wish I could do over."

"You're making her proud now," Ian said.

"I hope so." Jeffrey picked up his cup and finished the last of his coffee. "Are we ready to move on? The guys are going to be waiting."

Ian chewed up the last of the bear claw, guzzled his coffee and gathered up the wet napkins. "Let's go."

Dave exited the cafe and stood waiting by Ian's car. "What's Lizzie doing for her bachelorette party?"

"She had a spa day and slumber party last Saturday."

"Sorry I wasn't here for that. It would have been fun to sneak over and scare the girls. Remember when we did that to Cindy Tanner?"

Ian chuckled as he ducked into the car. "We were sixteen then, I think we've matured a little since then."

"Maybe you have," Dave countered. "Cindy didn't speak to either of us for the rest of the year."

"No, but I seem to recall you got Jenny Grimley's phone number that night. Whatever happened to Jenny and Cindy?"

The two men reminisced about high school friends the rest of the drive to the restaurant.

CHAPTER FORTY-FIVE

"Come on, Colin. We're going to be late," Cassandra called from the doorway of the hotel room.

"I'm coming." Colin entered the sitting room, looping his tie around his neck. A minute later, the couple stepped out into the hallway and started toward the elevator.

"What are you still doing here?" Cassandra exclaimed when she saw Lizzie in the concierge lounge.

Lizzie looked up, her tired eyes meeting Cassandra's. "I'm leaving in a few minutes. We have some VIPs checking in; they should have been here an hour ago, but their flight was delayed."

"Isn't there anyone else who can take care of that?" Cassandra was concerned by Lizzie's appearance. Her face was pale and her hands appeared to be shaking.

"Ben will be here for the check-in. I just wanted to make sure the amenities they requested were set up." Lizzie straightened a floral arrangement on the table in the center of the lounge and stepped toward Cassandra.

"You two go ahead. I'll be right behind you. You have directions to the church, right?"

"We do," Colin assured her as he touched Cassandra's shoulder and guided her away from the lounge.

"Don't stay too long, dear," Cassandra called.

The elevator opened a minute after Colin pushed the button and Cassandra followed him inside. "You don't think she's having second thoughts about this, do you?"

Colin pressed the lobby button then leaned back against the wall. "No, I don't. I think she's dedicated to her work and is about to take the longest break from it she's ever had. I imagine she's worried about all the things that can go wrong while she's gone. Remember how anxious she was in

Vermont? That was only a long weekend and it was obvious she thought about calling to check-in every day."

Cassandra nodded. "You're right. I'm being a nervous mother of the groom."

The elevator doors opened and they stepped out; turning the corner into the lobby, they almost crashed into Stephen.

"Did you see Lizzie upstairs?" He was out breath and his tie was crooked.

"Yes, she was in the lounge."

"Thanks." He dashed off toward the elevators.

"I hope everything's all right," Cassandra fretted. "Should we go back up?"

"I'm sure everything is fine. Stephen's probably trying to make sure she gets to the rehearsal on time." They stepped outside and a valet greeted them, opening the passenger door for Cassandra.

She ducked inside and Colin soon slid into the driver's seat. "I have a bad feeling, Colin."

"Relax. If she's a few minutes late, it won't be the end of the world." Colin waved to the valet and pulled away from the hotel.

CHAPTER FORTY-SIX

When the elevator doors opened on the concierge floor, Stephen ran down the short corridor to the lounge. The room was empty, but he heard noises in the pantry area. He pushed through the narrow door and found Lizzie riffling through the refrigerator.

"What are you looking for?"

"I know there is a fresh wedge of Jarlsberg cheese in here. I ordered it last week for the Lachey family. That's the only thing missing from their list of requests. I received a text alert that the flight landed ten minutes ago."

Stephen stepped forward and pulled her away from the refrigerator, then reached up to a compartment on the door that was rarely used. He pulled out the wedge of cheese and handed it to her. "I didn't want Ben or Jessica to put it out by accident. Now you need to leave for the rehearsal."

"I know. I'm on my way." She took the cheese, removed it from its wrapping and started slicing it.

Stephen ran a hand through his hair, realizing he'd done so more than a dozen times in the past ten minutes. How was he going to tell Lizzie the news? "Before you go, there's something I need to tell you."

"Sure, what is it?" Lizzie had finished slicing the cheese and was now arranging it on a decorative cheese board, adding some fresh strawberries and crackers.

Stephen watched her finish the tray, cover it, and set it in the refrigerator. How could she be so calm and focused when her wedding rehearsal was scheduled to start in half an hour? It would take almost twenty minutes to get to the church from the hotel and he couldn't imagine she was going in her work clothes.

"I'll let Ben know it's in here on my way out. What did you need to talk about?" Lizzie moved back into the lounge and Stephen knew her critical gaze was making a final sweep of the room.

"Maybe you should sit down." He moved toward a pair of comfortable wingback chairs and took a seat himself, waiting for her to get settled.

"You sound serious. You aren't leaving the hotel before I get back, are you?" The panic in her eyes made his chest constrict.

"No, nothing like that."

She relaxed and smiled. "That's good to hear. I think Ian would kill me if I told him I couldn't go on our honeymoon."

Stephen started to run his hand through his hair again, then dropped his hand to his tie, which he straightened. He reached into his jacket pocket and pulled out a cell phone that he extended to her. "You left your phone on your desk. There was a call and I saw it was from the caterer so I answered it. They had a fire this morning. They aren't going to be able to do your reception."

When he'd heard the news he was sure his heart had stopped beating for a full minute, so he couldn't imagine what was happening inside Lizzie now. He held his breath, waiting for her to speak.

"I should call Ian and let him know I'm going to be late." She started to dial, but Stephen reached out and took the phone from her.

"You go to the rehearsal. I'll handle this."

Lizzie reached for the phone. "Why do I need to practice walking down an aisle? Emma can stand in for me and everyone else can practice their walk; I can't have a reception without food."

"I'll talk to Chef Gustave and call some of the Concierge Club members. I'm sure we can put together a menu similar to what you had planned." Stephen stood and pulled Lizzie to her feet. "Go to the church and leave this with me."

Lizzie bit her lip, then looked him in the eyes. "Are you sure?"

"I have the same resources you do. I can do this."

She nodded and pulled him into a tight hug. "Thank you."

He felt his face flush with heat as they separated. "You need to get going."

"Be sure to call Patricia. She has the most contacts in the food and beverage end of the business."

"I know." He walked her to the elevator. "I'm sure we'll have this worked out in no time."

"You're supposed to come to dinner after the rehearsal."

"Cassandra gave me the details. Don't wait for me, though. I'll get there as soon as I can."

They stepped into the lobby a few minutes later and Stephen could still see the concern on Lizzie's face. This wasn't the way to start the wedding weekend, but things happen when you least expect them. He'd learned that over the past year.

He followed her into the front office, where she collected her purse and made sure her computer was turned off.

"Don't worry. I promise this will work out. I'll see you in a couple of hours." He gave her a gentle push out the door.

Lizzie's only response was a nod before she started across the lobby. Stephen watched until she turned a corner then raced back to his desk, dialing his cell phone as he sat down.

CHAPTER FORTY-SEVEN

Lizzie moved through the service corridor, passed through the doors of the loading dock and made her way to her car. Her mind was in a tug of war; one side numb with shock, the other racing with questions. How could Stephen pull together food for a hundred people in less than twenty-four hours? All the caterers in the city were certain to be booked with Christmas parties. She shouldn't be leaving Stephen alone. She was on her way back into the hotel when her cell phone rang with Ian's ring tone, the Michael Bolton song, "Soul Provider".

"Hey, sweetheart. Are you okay? Mom said you were stressed about some VIP arrival."

"The caterers had a fire and won't be able to do the reception." As she said it, she felt detached from the situation, like she was speaking about someone else's wedding.

"Oh no, how are we going to find another caterer this late?"

"Stephen's working on it." She closed her car door and started the engine. "I'm leaving for the church now. Maybe you can get Pastor Donovan to lead a prayer before I get there."

"Lizzie, are you sure you're all right to drive? You don't sound like yourself."

"I'm a nervous wreck, but I know Stephen will find a way to fix this. I'll see you soon." She ended the call and pulled out onto the road, praying she'd make it to the church safely.

She'd missed most of the Friday night traffic leaving downtown and pulled into the church parking lot a little less than twenty minutes later. Ian was sitting on the curb and jumped up the moment she'd parked.

"I guess it's a good thing I didn't ask Stephen to be one of my groomsmen after all," Ian joked when he met her.

"I feel like I should be back at the hotel with him." She leaned into Ian's embrace.

"If anyone in this town can manage this crisis as well as you, it's Stephen." Ian tilted her face up to his. "And you said all that really matters is a big cake and dancing, right? We still have those things even if the food changes."

She couldn't help but smile. Chef Gustave had banned her from the Hotel Lago kitchen for the entire week so there would be no chance of her seeing the cake as each component was made. "As long as I have you, I'm happy. Everyone else," she shrugged, "I guess they will have to make do with whatever Stephen can scrounge up. Even if it's just peanut butter and jelly sandwiches."

Ian wrapped his arm around her shoulders and walked them toward the chapel. "I know you want me to believe this is no big deal, but inside you're still freaking out."

"Maybe I can skip dinner tonight and go help Stephen."

"If you think that's what you need to do, I will make sure everyone else understands."

They reached the chapel and Ian pulled the door open for her. The sound of several conversations came to a complete stop the minute they stepped inside.

"Sorry I'm late. Last day of work always seems to take forever."

Stephanie, Emma, Mona, and Cassandra all swarmed around Lizzie, each asking how they could help and if she was all right. She assured them all was well and Stephen had everything under control then turned to Pastor Donovan.

"Thank you for the prayer, pastor. I think we are ready to get started now."

"Of course. Ian, come stand up here." The pastor started placing Ian and his groomsmen while his wife took the ladies to the back of the church and reviewed their order of entrance.

A few minutes later, an iPod playing the processional music started and the ladies made their way to the front of the church. Lizzie clung to Ron's arm, waiting for her own turn. When the music changed to the wedding march, she felt him squeeze her arm and turned to smile at him. They moved together, each step precise and in sync. Her gaze moved from Dave to Jeffrey to Ian, across Pastor Donovan to Stephanie and Mona. Emma and Cassandra stood across from each other in the first row of pews, both women beaming with delight. If this was only the practice, how much brighter would all of those faces look tomorrow for the real thing?

Ron kissed her on the cheek before passing her over to Ian. Pastor Donovan reviewed the order of the service, making sure they understood when they would need to move onto the platform for the lighting of the unity candle and communion.

"Then you will be able to kiss your bride," Pastor Donovan said.

Ian leaned forward and gave Lizzie a long, tender kiss. She heard Stephanie and Mona giggling.

"It looks like you have that part down," the pastor said.

Lizzie stepped back and grinned. "We'd hate to bump heads during the actual ceremony. Don't want to embarrass ourselves."

"I think you'll do fine." Pastor Donovan winked at them. "Unless anyone has questions, I think we are done. Who's ready to eat?"

Everyone fell out of line and moved toward the door. Lizzie found her purse and retrieved her phone, but there were no missed calls from Stephen.

"You go back to the hotel," Ian said. "If you need anything, call."

"I'll try to make it to the restaurant for dessert." She kissed him and hurried out to her car.

CHAPTER FORTY-EIGHT

A valet opened the door when Lizzie pulled to a stop in front of Hotel Lago. "I thought your rehearsal was tonight."

"All rehearsed," she said. "Keep the car close if you can." She hurried inside and found Stephen at his desk, cell phone to one ear and desk phone to the other.

"Hold on, Lizzie just walked in." He set both phones on the desk. "What are you doing here?"

"We can accomplish more together. When you finish those calls you can catch me up." She moved to her office and found a fresh legal pad.

"You should be at dinner," Stephen said when he entered the office a few minutes later.

"I think making sure there is a dinner tomorrow night is a bit more important. Who have you talked to?"

Stephen referred to a notebook he'd brought in with him. "Chef Gustave is calling in a few of the cooks who had the night off and they are going to handle side items. Patricia has a call out to her cooks to see who can help out. She should be getting back to me in the next half hour. I called Maggie at Avalon Grove and she is checking to see if anyone there is willing to come in and help. She's also checking to see if they have enough servingware on hand. Do you still want to go with a buffet? I should have asked you that before you left earlier."

"I think the buffet will be easiest. Did the caterer say anything about if their staff will still be available?" Lizzie fished in her purse for her phone. "I should have called them after you gave me the message. What was I thinking?"

"I imagine you were in shock. You took the news better than I expected. There wasn't any mention of the staff. I was told there had been a fire and they didn't know when the fire department would allow them back into the building, so they wouldn't be able to provide for your reception."

Lizzie shook her head and reached for her rolodex, flipping through the cards without even reading them. "I knew things were going too well."

Stephen reached across the desk and stilled Lizzie's hand. "You and Chef provided a reception meal for Mr. and Mrs. Singh during a hurricane with only emergency power and a skeleton crew. This is going to be a piece of cake."

She took several deep breaths and leaned back in her chair. "You're right, and it sounds like you've already accomplished quite a bit."

Stephen's cell phone rang. "Hey, Patricia. I have you on speaker phone with Lizzie."

"Oh, Lizzie, I'm so sorry this happened, but Stephen's on top of it. Aren't you supposed to be at your rehearsal right now?"

"We finished rehearsal. Everyone's at dinner right now."

"Let me tell you where we stand so you can get to dinner, then. I have a dozen guys who volunteered to help out. They will be here tomorrow morning. My head chef is working on finding enough chicken and roast beef."

"If he can't find those, turkey would be fine," Lizzie chimed in. "I didn't want people to feel like they were having an early Christmas dinner, but I can't be too picky now."

"I'll let him know," Patricia said. "James has put a call out to all the servers at City Walk to see if anyone would be willing to pitch in. I told him to call Stephen if he gets any response. Do you need table linens?"

"No, I rented those through a company we use here at Hotel Lago. They are being delivered to Avalon Grove in the morning."

"It sounds like all we are waiting on is the meat for the carving station and a final count on servers," Stephen said.

"Let me know if I can do anything else," Patricia offered.

"Thanks, I appreciate all you've done." Lizzie's heart had been racing since leaving the church but now slowed, and she sent up a silent prayer of thanks for the wonderful friends God had placed in her life.

Stephen ended the call and set the phone on the desk. "See, it's under control. Go to dinner."

"Only if you come with me." Lizzie stood. "When I designated you my wedding fire fighter, I had no idea an actual fire would be involved."

"I'm just glad you weren't having a plated dinner with specific requests for chicken or fish. I think that would have been harder to pull together." Stephen followed her out of the office.

"I want to stop and thank Chef before we leave."

"You aren't allowed in the kitchen," Stephen reminded her. "Why don't you wait until tomorrow? I imagine he's busy right now trying to find everything he will need for the side dishes."

"You're right. I don't want to get in his way and make him regret helping out. Do you know how to get to the restaurant?"

Stephen nodded. "See you there."

Lizzie watched him move off toward the service hallway before exiting out the front door.

"Sorry to hear about your caterer," one of the valets said when she stepped outside.

Her car was still in the porte cochere and the valet walked her to it, opening the door for her. Despite the immense number of hospitality jobs in Orlando, she knew how interconnected they were and news traveled fast in the industry.

"Thanks. Stephen's done a great job organizing a replacement squad."

"He's a smart guy," the valet said. "I hope you have a wonderful day tomorrow and enjoy your time off."

"You all stay out of trouble while I'm gone, and Merry Christmas."

The valet winked as he shut the door and stepped back. Lizzie found her keys still in the ignition and wondered how they had known her visit would be so short.

She waved to the valet and put the car in gear. Her stomach growled and she realized how hungry she was. The thought of Arnaldo's cooking spurred her on.

CHAPTER FORTY-NINE

Half an hour later, Lizzie parked and waited for Stephen to pull in beside her. The smell of garlic and rosemary filled her nostrils when she opened her door. Stephen jumped out of his SUV and came around the car to meet her.

"It smells great. I forgot to have lunch today," he said, rubbing his stomach.

"Me too. Have you eaten here before?"

"No. Eating out for me is usually fast food or a sports bar with Jeffrey."

"You're going to love it. Between Ian and I, we've tried almost everything on the menu."

Stephen pulled open the door for her, then followed her inside. A cheer arose when they entered and Ian popped to his feet, hurrying to greet them. Lizzie tilted her head up to accept his kiss, then snuggled into his side while he shook Stephen's hand.

"Thanks for helping out, Stephen." Ian walked them to a large table set up in the middle of the restaurant.

"Just doing the task Lizzie assigned me," Stephen quipped.

"I'm glad she didn't ask me to put together an entire meal in less than twenty-four hours," Stephanie said. "I'm having a hard enough time coming up with a toast."

Everyone laughed and chairs were rearranged to make room for Lizzie and Stephen. Before Lizzie could be seated, though, Arnaldo appeared from the kitchen. He kissed her on both cheeks then stood back and held both her hands.

"I was so very sorry to learn about the caterer. Fire is a constant fear in this business, but we often get complacent about it. If there is anything you need, you let me know."

"Thank you, Arnaldo. I'm grateful for the support we've received."

"Now, sit, enjoy your dinner. I can hear your stomach rumbling." Arnaldo slid out a chair for her and Lizzie sat down. Half-eaten salads sat in front of all the guests.

"Can I skip the salad and go straight to the appetizer?"

Arnaldo nodded and returned to the kitchen.

Lizzie looked around the table, enjoying the sight of her friends together. She glanced toward the other end of the table where Dave and Jeffrey were seated next to each other, deep in conversation. Dave let out a bellow of laughter then covered his mouth and looked around in embarrassment.

"I take it they worked things out," she whispered to Ian.

"I took them to coffee before dinner last night. Jeffrey apologized and the rest of the night Dave warmed up to him. I don't know if Dave ever apologized for his behavior, but Jeffrey doesn't seem to mind."

A team of servers arrived to clear away the salads and replace them with appetizer platters. Cassandra had decided to go with a set menu to help keep the meal moving along and minimize the work for the kitchen staff. When another large group reservation had cancelled a few days earlier, Arnaldo had been gracious enough to move the party to a seating at eight fifteen.

The guests complimented each course and dessert was greeted with a mixture of delight and groans of overstuffed stomachs. Lizzie didn't think she could eat another bite until a small plate was set in front of her, upon which sat an enticing slice of lemon cake with a fluffy lemon icing. She took one bite and felt like she was eating a lemon flavored cloud.

Pastor Donovan stood and conversations quieted as he raised his coffee cup. "Before we all leave tonight, I'd like to make a toast to Ian and Lizzie. It's been an honor and a blessing for me and my wife to get to know you. From the day Ian proposed at the front of the church, I've seen the love between you blossom and deepen. I firmly believe God set you apart for each other and, though you've gone through some valleys, both separately and together, you've remained true to each other. I pray you will have many years of happiness together."

Glasses were clinked together around the table, then the ringing of silverware on glass filled the restaurant until Ian leaned over and kissed Lizzie. She didn't mind that everyone watched them.

"All right, enough already, save some for tomorrow," Jeffrey yelled, accompanied by laughter.

"Sixteen more hours," Ian whispered in her ear before pulling his head away.

Lizzie felt her stomach tighten, then flutter. This time tomorrow she would be Mrs. Ian Cavanaugh and she couldn't imagine anything better.

CHAPTER FIFTY

One by one, the guests started to leave, stopping to hug Ian and Lizzie, confirming the times they needed to be at the church in the morning. Jeffrey pulled Lizzie aside while Stephen and Stephanie were talking with Ian and Colin.

"You know how happy I am for you, right?" Jeffrey locked eyes with her.

"I do and I'm grateful for your support when I wasn't so sure of things."

"I think part of me knew the first night I introduced the two of you that you were meant for each other. I'm sorry I didn't make it easy at first."

Lizzie shook her head. "You don't have anything to apologize for. If it hadn't been for you, we wouldn't be here tonight. I hope one day you can find happiness again."

"After Camylle died I didn't think I'd ever be happy again, but I am. You changed my life and every day I find something new to be thankful for." Jeffrey glanced over his shoulder. Lizzie followed his gaze and saw Ian was alone. Jeffrey waved for him to join them.

"I have something to tell you, but it's been impossible to get the two of you together this week." Jeffrey rubbed his hands together and Lizzie could feel the excitement radiating from him.

"Well, you have us now, what's going on?" Ian asked.

"It's Michelle. She accepted Christ on Sunday."

"That's wonderful," Lizzie exclaimed, pulling Jeffrey into a bear hug. She felt Ian join the hug, wrapping one arm around her and the other around Jeffrey.

"That's great news," Ian said.

Lizzie let go and stepped back. "You have to tell us all about it."

"I'll tell you when you get back from your honeymoon. It's getting late and you have a big day tomorrow."

"Yeah, I need to go home and get some beauty rest," Ian teased.

"Are you bringing Michelle to the wedding? Stephanie made me keep a place for her; said she was sure you would be bringing her."

Jeffrey grinned. "Not sure how Stephanie could have known since I wasn't planning on it, but she seems excited to be coming."

"Good, I can't wait to meet her."

After Jeffrey left, only Emma, Ron, Colin, and Cassandra remained. Lizzie wrapped her arm around Ian's waist and they returned to the table.

"You did good, mom." Ian kissed his mother's cheek.

"I couldn't have done it without Sheila."

"Why don't you two sit down for a minute?" Ron said. Lizzie stifled a yawn and sat down next to Emma. Ian sat next to her and she leaned her head on his shoulder.

"I know Emma and I aren't your parents, Lizzie, but you are like a daughter to us. It means a lot that you've included us in this wedding and we wanted to give the two of you a special gift." Ron pulled an envelope from his pocket.

Lizzie accepted it in trembling hands. "I love you guys and I couldn't imagine getting married without you." She opened the envelope and gasped.

Emma leaned forward. "I know how much you love the tea cup your mom bought on her honeymoon in Savannah. I was able to find a matching teapot and a set of cups. They arrived earlier this week, but I was afraid to bring them tonight. I didn't want them to get broken."

"They're beautiful," Lizzie murmured as she handed a photo of the tea set to Ian.

"What a wonderful gift," Cassandra said.

"Ian, you've always made us proud," his father said, "and we are thrilled you are bringing Lizzie into our family. We look forward to watching all of the things God is going to do in your lives. We have a gift for you as well, but it won't be here until you get back from your trip to..."

"Good one, dad. I'm not spilling any information."

Colin shrugged. "I had to try. Anyway, we know how much you and Lizzie enjoy home improvement projects."

Ian groaned and Lizzie giggled.

"So we bought you all the things you'll need for an outdoor kitchen. They'll be delivered after the first of the year."

"Thank you both," Lizzie said. "We are blessed to have the four of you watching over us."

"There's one more thing." Cassandra reached into her purse and pulled out a small box. "This is just for Lizzie."

"You didn't have to do that," Lizzie said, accepting the box. She untied the ribbon and lifted the lid. The moment she saw the gift inside her eyes filled with tears. She lifted out a small picture frame that held a photo of her parents taken at a Valentine's Day party a week before they died. It was a photo she knew well; she carried a copy of it in her wallet.

"I saw the frame when Emma and I were shopping. Emma helped me get the photo. The clasp on it can be used on a charm bracelet or necklace, but I thought you could clip it to your bouquet so you can know they are with you."

Lizzie felt Ian's arm on her shoulders and leaned into him. Ron pulled a handkerchief from his pocket and passed it across the table. She wiped at the tears now flowing down her face, then reached for Cassandra's hand. "Thank you."

CHAPTER FIFTY-ONE

With each passing moment the sun crept higher, bathing the neighborhood in pure, golden light. Lizzie sat on the front porch, an empty cup of coffee cradled in her hand, a fleece blanket and thick bathrobe protecting her from an unusual chill in the air. She'd woken at five and been unable to fall back asleep. At six thirty, she'd given up trying and made a pot of coffee, which she'd enjoyed on the front porch as she read through the book of Psalms.

"Good morning."

Lizzie looked up and smiled at the white-haired lady climbing the porch steps. "Good morning, Mae. You're up early."

"The older I get the earlier I wake up. Are you excited about the wedding?"

"I can't believe it's happening."

Mae took a seat next to Lizzie, her clear, blue eyes twinkling. "I knew Ian was a special man the first night I met him. He was so concerned when he'd finished working on your floors and left the key with me."

"You never mentioned that before. What was he concerned about?"

"He didn't say, but I could see it in his face. I've raised two boys, remember, I can tell when they are worried."

Lizzie grimaced. "We didn't have an argument, exactly, but I was hurt and angry." She gave a wry laugh. "I should have known then communication was going to be a problem for us."

"You had some difficult spots, but God uses those times to draw us closer to Him. You've learned valuable lessons from each other and I have faith you will continue to grow together."

"You've been a wonderful neighbor and friend; always looking out for me since the first day I met you." Lizzie reached for Mae's hand.

"I've enjoyed watching you bring life back to this old house." Mae stood. "I better go so you can think about getting ready."

"I'll see you at the church." Lizzie watched her friend amble across the street to her home and waved when Mae looked back before closing her front door, then Lizzie gathered her things and retreated inside herself.

The ceremony was at two, leaving her all morning to prepare, and for her nerves to rattle her. She set her empty cereal bowl on the coffee table and curled into a ball, tucking herself into the corner of the couch, as if this would protect her from the swirl of emotions. A knock on the door startled her.

"Lizzie, it's me," Ian's voice came through the door. "I know I'm not supposed to see you before the wedding but I figured you would be awake. I didn't sleep much myself."

She moved to the door and pressed her cheek against it. "You aren't having second thoughts, are you?"

Ian laughed. "Not on your life." He stopped laughing and became serious. "Are you?"

"No," she whispered. She placed her hand on the doorknob, wanting to see his face, to fall into his arms and absorb his strength.

"You sound like you need a hug."

It was the tenderness in his voice that broke all her will power. "Close your eyes. I'm going to open the door."

"They're closed."

She closed her own, pulled open the door and stepped into his embrace. The steady beat of his heart and the fresh scent of his skin quieted the warring thoughts within her. "You always know when I need you."

"That's my job and I take it very seriously." He stroked her hair and she felt the tension in her shoulders melt away.

"Aren't you taking the boys out for breakfast?"

"I have time. We aren't meeting until nine and they'll understand if I'm a few minutes late."

"I'm glad they seem to have worked things out between them. I like Dave."

"He's a good guy. I wish we could see each other more often."

"Mmhmm," Lizzie murmured. They stood in silence for several more minutes and she wondered if Ian had needed this as much as she had.

Ian broke the silence with a prayer: "Dear Lord, I thank you for bringing Lizzie into my life. I thank you for bringing us through some difficult times and making our love stronger for it. I pledge to love her as you love us, and to keep you at the center of our relationship. I pray Your hand will always guide us and that all we do will bring glory and honor to you. Be with us on this special day as we are joined together in marriage and bless all those who have come to celebrate this moment with us. In Your holy, precious name I pray, Amen."

"Amen," Lizzie echoed. She squeezed him tight and felt him squeeze in return. "You should get a move on."

He kissed the top of her head. "See you in a few hours."

Lizzie stepped back inside and closed the door, resting her forehead against its cool surface. She waited until she heard his car start, the engine soon fading into the distance, then she opened her eyes and stood up straight. Any questions she may have had had vanished; this was the man she was meant to spend the rest of her life with. Slowly, a smile crept across her face and she twirled on the smooth wood floor.

CHAPTER FIFTY-TWO

A few minutes before eleven, Lizzie pulled to a stop in the church parking lot. A white delivery van was parked by the curb, and she smiled when she saw her friend Jackson, the owner of Fields of Bloom. Three of his assistants were busy unloading flowers under his watchful eye.

"They're gorgeous," Lizzie said as she approached the van.

"Only the best for you."

"I'm sure you say that to all of your brides." She kissed him on the cheek.

"Let me help you with that." He grimaced as he transferred the duffel bag from her shoulder to his own. "Are you planning on moving in?"

"You know me, always prepared for every eventuality."

"Is there a replacement groom in here?"

"That's the one thing I don't have to worry about. A shoe strap breaking, lipstick melting, curlers overheating, those are my real concerns."

Jackson shook his head. "You are the most organized person I know. Come on, let's get you inside."

Lizzie led him to a side door that opened into a room with three vanity tables, a full-length mirror and a small wet bar area. A pitcher of orange juice, a plate of cheese and an assortment of fruit were displayed on the bar with a card addressed to Lizzie. After hanging her dress on a wall hook, she opened the card.

A little something to hold you over until the reception.
Be sure to check the refrigerator.
Love, Ella & Bill Donovan

"That's sweet," she said.

Jackson set the duffel bag on a small sofa and wandered over to the bar. "Is that all you're eating before the wedding?"

"I hadn't even thought about it. With photos and everything, we probably won't make it to the reception until four. Of course, I'm so nervous I don't even know if I can eat."

Her stomach rumbled and Jackson chuckled. "Sounds like your stomach thinks otherwise."

"Knock, knock." Emma pushed open the door and stepped inside. She carried her own garment bag and a small overnight case. "Jackson, it's good to see you."

"You too, Emma. I better get back to work, though. We should have everything set up within the hour."

"Will you come get me when you're finished? I'm afraid I'll be too nervous walking down the aisle to appreciate all the hard work you guys are doing."

"Sure thing. See you in a bit."

When Jackson was gone, Lizzie opened her duffel bag and removed items, placing them on the vanity furthest from the door. Emma wandered over to the wet bar and plucked a handful of grapes from a crystal bowl.

"This is thoughtful. Is it from the church?"

"The pastor and his wife. They've been so kind to us."

Emma opened the dorm-size refrigerator and laughed. "Did you happen to mention to them how much you like spinach dip?"

"Not that I remember. Why?"

Emma lifted a bowl filled with homemade spinach dip and set it on the counter.

"Mm, I could eat that whole thing." Lizzie reached for one of the crackers on the cheese tray and dipped it into the bowl. "That's good."

"I hope you brought your toothbrush," Emma said.

"Of course I did. You didn't think I was going to kiss my groom without fresh breath, did you?"

"Who doesn't have fresh breath?" Stephanie closed the door behind her and dropped the tote bag she was carrying at her feet.

"No one," Lizzie said. "Emma's giving me a hard time about enjoying this spinach dip Ella left for us."

"Let me have some. I'm famished. I was so worried about forgetting something I forgot to eat breakfast."

"Dig in," Lizzie said. "Was there anything else in the fridge, Emma?"

"Some bottles of water."

The door opened again and Mona entered in a flurry. "Sorry I'm late."

"You're fine. Come in and put your things down." Lizzie sat down at her vanity and organized her supplies. She checked the wall for a power outlet and found one on the left side of the table. Untangling the cord for her hot rollers, she plugged them in and set them on the corner of the table to warm up.

Stephanie carried a small plate filled with dip, crackers and fruit to the vanity by the door and unpacked her own bag while Mona poured herself a glass of orange juice.

Emma unzipped her garment bag and removed her dress. "Is Cassandra getting dressed here or at the hotel?"

"I invited her to join us, but she had an appointment at the hotel salon to get her hair done."

"I wish I had thought to make an appointment for my hair." Mona lifted a limp lock of it. "I can never make it do anything."

"Don't worry. I'll take care of it," Stephanie said. "My sister is a hair dresser and I've picked up a few tricks from her."

There was a knock on the door followed by Jackson asking, "Is everyone decent?"

"Come in, Jackson." Lizzie stood and grabbed a few grapes.

"You ready to see what we've done?"

"Lead the way." Lizzie followed him out with the rest of the girls behind her. They went around to the front of the chapel and Jackson pulled open the door, stepping aside so they could all pass through.

The chapel, which was already a beautiful setting with its nativity stained-glass and polished wooden pews, now reminded Lizzie of an elegant woman, dressed for a ball. Kissing balls of white hydrangeas adorned every other pew. The communion table was draped with garlands accented with bows made from Christmas plaid ribbon. Two large vases filled with red roses, purple hydrangea, and dusty miller flanked the unity candle. In each of the six windows, small square vases held a sprig of fir, a white hydrangea and a miniature version of the purple ornaments being used for the place card holders at the reception.

"It's perfect," Lizzie whispered. She turned to find Jackson and his assistants at the back of the chapel, beaming. "Thank you so much."

"I have your bouquets in the van. Do you want me to give you the boutonnieres as well?"

"That would be fine. Emma can deliver them to the guys when they arrive."

Jackson nodded and motioned for his assistants to follow him out. Lizzie took another couple of minutes to admire the work, drinking it all in so she would remember every detail. She grinned when she noticed Jackson had used a thin version of the Christmas plaid ribbon to hang the poofs. She loved the plaid, but hadn't wanted it to overpower the decorations. She didn't want to have cliché Christmas decor, but had given in to little nods to the season with the ornaments, ribbon, and garland.

Emma touched Lizzie on the shoulder. "We better get back to our room. Ian should be here soon."

Lizzie glanced at her watch, surprised to see it was already twelve thirty. Only ninety minutes to show time. She took one last look around the chapel and followed her friends outside.

One of the floral assistants waved at them from the van before climbing into the driver's seat. Lizzie waved back then turned the corner toward the side door. Jackson was coming out as they approached.

"Your bouquets are all set. Leave them in the water until you're ready to walk down the aisle." He leaned in to give her a hug. "Time for me to get home and change. See you at the reception."

The subtle scent of the flowers greeted them as they opened the door. Lizzie moved to the table where three vases held the delicate creations. She smiled when she saw Jackson had wrapped the stems of each bouquet in the Christmas plaid ribbon. She reached for her own bouquet, a pair of white hydrangeas with purple irises woven into them, surrounded by tree fern for a whimsical finish. The remaining two bouquets were purple and white tulips with lily grass.

"That Jackson does good work," Emma said.

"Yes, he does. I can't imagine using any other florist. I've never received a single complaint from any of our guests when we use his flowers for arrangements."

"If the curlers are ready, I can start on your hair," Emma offered.

"Oh, I forgot to even bring curlers," Mona cried.

"Don't worry." Lizzie smiled and opened her duffel bag. "I have an extra set."

"Were you a girl scout as a kid?" Stephanie took the curlers and plugged them in.

"No, but after a couple of incidents of not being prepared for the unexpected, I've learned my lesson. That's part of the reason it's been driving me crazy that Ian won't tell me where we are going on our honeymoon. How can I be prepared?"

Stephanie grinned. "Maybe that's part of his plan."

Lizzie gave her friend a playful punch before sitting down in front of her mirror. "I wish I'd gotten more sleep last night. Covering these dark circles is going to be difficult."

Emma snapped her fingers and moved to the refrigerator. "Ella thought of that too."

She removed a small plate of cucumber slices and handed it to Lizzie. "Once I get your hair rolled up, you can lay down on the couch and place these on your eyes. They will help reduce the inflammation that causes the dark color."

"I wonder how many brides Ella has done this for. She's like a wedding angel."

"All right, turn around now so I can finish your hair."

CHAPTER FIFTY-THREE

"I feel fit for battle after that meal." Jeffrey patted his stomach as he followed Colin, Ian, and Dave out of the restaurant.

"Well, I hope there's no need for battle today." Ian unlocked his car and opened the door.

"I have to run back to the hotel to pick up your mother," Colin said. "Is there anything you need me to do on the way to the church?"

"No, I'm good. Dave, are you going back to the hotel as well?"

"Yeah, I need to pick up my tux."

"All right, but don't take too long."

"There are hours until the wedding," Jeffrey said.

"I know, but I don't want anything to delay the ceremony."

"Don't worry. We'll be there with plenty of time to spare," Colin assured him as he closed the door to his rental car.

Ian watched them pull out of the parking lot then turned to Jeffrey. "Can you believe it's finally the big day?"

Jeffrey grinned. "It does seem like you have been together forever. I hope you know how happy I am for the two of you."

"I do, and I appreciate the way you made peace with Dave."

"It was the right thing to do. I don't want any of the stuff from my old life hanging over me."

"I have to say, I'm impressed with how you've been growing in your faith."

"Getting involved with the men's group at church seemed to make a lot of pieces fall into place."

"That's good to hear. We all need a support group we can rely on."

"Speaking of support, I was surprised Stephen wasn't here this morning."

Ian grimaced. "Me too. He texted and said he was still working on the food for the reception."

"Does Lizzie know that?"

"I don't think so."

"Last night it sounded like everything was under control."

"That's what I thought too. Maybe he's just trying to coordinate how everything is going to be delivered to the Inn."

"So, what are you going to do for the next couple of hours?"

"I have a couple of things I need to finalize for the honeymoon."

"Isn't it a little late for that?"

"No, these are just a few little things. I don't think it will take more than half an hour then I will head to the church."

"All right. I'll see you there then."

"Be there by twelve forty-five."

"I will. I just want to make sure Michelle knows how to get there. I feel weird not picking her up, but there's no reason for her to have to sit around for an hour while we all get ready." Jeffrey headed off to his truck on the other side of the parking lot and Ian ducked into his car.

He checked the center console to make sure he still had the key Emma had given him, then put the car in drive and headed for Lizzie's house.

When he pulled into the driveway, he noticed Lizzie's neighbor Mae in her rocking chair across the street. He jogged across and smiled down at her. "You're looking lovely today."

"Thank you, dear. Do you want to sit down for a minute?"

"I wish I could, but I have to take care of few things before I head to the church. Are your boys picking you up for the wedding?"

"Yes, Liam will be here around one."

"Good, we'll see you there." He leaned down and kissed her cheek. "Thank you for being such a good friend to Lizzie. I know she thinks the world of you."

"She's an impressive young woman. It's nice to see her so happy. You take good care of her."

"Yes, ma'am, I will." Ian hurried across the street and into the house.

He felt strange to be here alone, almost like an intruder. Everything was in perfect order, as if she had prepared for entertaining before leaving this morning. In her bedroom, he found two suitcases next to the window seat on the far side of the room. He lifted them onto the bed and opened each one. She'd used packing cubes to help shrink down her clothes and maximize the space in the bag. He opened one to determine what type of clothes were inside. When he found several pairs of shorts, he closed the cube, returned it to the suitcase and placed the case under the bed.

He carried the remaining bag from the bedroom to the living room, then returned to the den. Here, he rummaged through the desk drawer where he'd found her passport before and tucked it into his pocket. Satisfied he had everything he needed, he carried the suitcase out to his car. One more stop, then he could head for the church.

CHAPTER FIFTY-FOUR

Outside, the sound of car doors closing and excited chatter had ended ten minutes earlier. Lizzie paced between the wet bar and her vanity table, careful to keep her gown off the floor. The clock on the wall read five minutes past two.

"I'm sure everything is fine," Stephanie said. "Maybe Ian's having trouble with his hair."

Lizzie wanted to laugh, but her throat felt as if it were held by a boa constrictor. The door opened and Ella Donovan stepped inside.

"How are you doing, Lizzie?"

"What's wrong, Ella? Is Ian okay?"

Ella nodded. "He is; all the guys are. They had a bit of a problem with a zipper and something about a damaged tie. Do you happen to have a safety pin?"

Lizzie felt her knees go weak with relief. She reached for the bar to steady herself and took a deep breath as the constriction in her throat released. "A wardrobe malfunction? Yes, of course I have safety pins."

She moved back to the vanity and reached for the duffel bag on the chair. She dug out a plastic pencil box that held several zippered bags. She found the one with safety pins and handed it to Ella.

"Ian said you'd be prepared. They should be ready in ten more minutes." Ella accepted the pins and slipped outside.

"You never think about the groom or groomsmen having trouble getting dressed." Mona sipped on a bottle of water.

"I told you there was nothing to worry about," Stephanie said.

"I know. Ian may be more excited about this wedding than I am."

Five minutes later there was a knock on the door before Ron stepped inside. "Your audience awaits."

Lizzie felt her heart flutter and her mouth went dry.

"I'm ready."

Stephanie, Mona, and Emma preceded her outside. Taking Ron's arm, Lizzie followed them along the path to the front of the chapel. Cassandra and Colin stood outside, their faces bright with excitement. The door opened and Stephen stepped out. With one look from him, relief washed over Lizzie. She hadn't even realized she'd been worried about the reception until he'd given her a small nod.

"We're all ready," Stephen said. "May I escort you in, Emma?"

"Thank you very much." Emma accepted his arm and stepped inside. Colin and Cassandra followed a few seconds later.

Flashing encouraging smiles at Lizzie, first Mona then Stephanie began their walk down the aisle. Now alone with Ron, Lizzie turned to look at the man who had taken on the role of her protector.

"Thank you for doing this, Ron." Lizzie fingered the picture frame she had attached to the ribbon around her bouquet.

"It's an honor. Your parents would be so proud of you."

She nodded, blinking back the tears that threatened. "No tears today. Let's get me married."

The moment the doors opened again, the music swelled to the wedding march. Ron squeezed her arm and they started down the aisle. She looked past the rows of guests and met Ian's gaze. She saw him straighten and lift his head higher, and felt her breath halt.

She felt a tug on her arm and realized she had stopped in the middle of the chapel. Ron leaned his head close and whispered, "Don't stop yet."

A nervous giggle escaped her as she took the next step. When they reached the front of the church, Ron placed Lizzie's hand in Ian's, kissed her on the cheek, then took a seat with Emma.

Pastor Donovan smiled down on them. "Let us open in prayer."

Lizzie met Ian's gaze before bowing her head and closing her eyes.

"Heavenly Father, we come to you this afternoon to celebrate the union of this couple."

She tried to concentrate on the prayer, but the pounding of her heart filled her ears. Ian squeezed her hand and she opened her eyes, realizing the prayer had ended. She met Ian's gaze, his eyes glistening with tears, and felt her own eyes start to water. Her heartbeat slowed and she could hear the pastor speaking again.

"Dearly beloved, we are gathered here today to join together Ian Fergal Cavanaugh and Elizabeth Christina Reynolds in holy matrimony." Pastor Donovan's words rang in Lizzie's ears, but her eyes never left Ian's.

"The day I watched Ian propose to Lizzie in front of the entire congregation, I hoped they would ask me to preside over their wedding, if only so I could get the whole story behind the surprising proposal. Getting to know them in preparation for this joyous day has shown me how they each embodied different aspects of the apostle Paul's description of love in First Corinthians Thirteen."

The pastor turned toward Lizzie. She tore her gaze away from Ian long enough to acknowledge Pastor Donovan. "Love does not envy, it does not boast, it is not proud. When I learned all Lizzie has overcome and all she has accomplished, and yet how humble she is about these things, I realized that even I could learn from her."

She blinked back tears and tried to smile at the pastor. He gave her a tiny nod before turning to Ian. "Love always protects, always trusts, always hopes, always perseveres. This is the perfect description of Ian and his love for Lizzie. It's not often I see young men with the instinct to protect and also to trust at the same time. I believe Ian's trust in both God and in Lizzie are what allowed them to overcome the obstacles they faced as a couple.

"I pray that the two of you will continue to grow in these characteristics and that they will strengthen your marriage for many years to come."

Lizzie agreed whole-heartedly. Ian's constant faith in her had given her the courage to trust herself in ways she hadn't before. It had allowed her to open her heart to him.

As the pastor moved on to the traditional vows, Lizzie watched Ian's lips move as he recited his own and tried to control the shaking of her hand as he placed the ring on her finger. Stephanie held out Ian's ring and Lizzie reached for it, but fumbled and watched it roll down the aisle.

Several chuckles could be heard around the chapel. Stephen hurried to catch the ring and brought it back to Lizzie.

"I, Elizabeth, take you, Ian, to be my husband. To have and to hold from this day forward, for better, for worse, for richer, for poorer, in sickness," Lizzie smiled at the memory of her recent illness, "and in health, to love and to cherish 'til death do us part."

The ring slid onto his finger and he clasped her hand in his as they ascended the steps onto the platform and lit the unity candle before moving to the communion table. A rich silence enveloped them as they took the elements together while the pianist softly played "The Lord's Prayer". They rose and faced each other, and Lizzie knew this moment would be imprinted on her memory forever.

"You may kiss the bride." Pastor Donovan smiled at them as he took a step back.

Ian leaned down and cupped her head in his hands. His lips were soft and warm. She closed her eyes, tasting salt and ranch dip. She thought of the snacks in her dressing room and wondered if Ella had arranged something similar for the groomsmen. Cheers and clapping filled the chapel as Ian released her and stepped back.

"May I present Mr. and Mrs. Ian Cavanaugh," Pastor Donovan said, bringing the congregation to their feet. Ian led Lizzie up the aisle, followed by Stephanie and Jeffrey, then Mona and Dave.

Outside the church, Ian lifted Lizzie off her feet and spun her around. "We did it, sweetheart."

She laughed and clung to him. "Be careful of the dress. I don't want to tear it before we get to the reception."

He set her down and hugs were shared between all of the wedding party before the guests started emerging from the church. Stephen made his way through the crowd and pulled Lizzie aside.

"I'm going to the Inn to make sure everything is set up. Chef called before the ceremony to let me know all the food had arrived."

"Thank you, Stephen. I don't know what I would have done without you."

Stephen flushed. "I'll see you over there."

CHAPTER FIFTY-FIVE

When the town car pulled up in front of the Avalon Grove Inn, Lizzie took a deep breath. Ian reached over and took her hand.

"I know you're worried about the food. Whatever happens, everyone will understand. I think they've all heard about the fire."

"I love that you know me so well, but I'm not worried."

"Then shall we go inside?"

"Ready when you are."

The driver came around the car and opened the door. Ian stepped out and held his hand out to Lizzie. She slid across the seat, holding her gown so it wouldn't drag along the ground. Ian escorted her to the door where Maggie, the catering manager, welcomed them.

"I can't wait for you to see the room," she said. "Your friend Jackson is an artist."

They paused at the entrance and Lizzie gasped. The room surpassed what she had imagined. The hardwood floor reflected the white lights wrapped around the exposed beams. The vases that had flanked the unity candle now decorated the buffet table.

The guest tables were covered with dove grey cloths accented with runners in the green, black and red of the Christmas plaid. The pomanders from the church had been placed in square glass vases for the centerpieces on the dinner tables and the bridal bouquets lined the head table. Delicate white plates rimed in silver, place card holders set in their center, silver-sprayed pinecones alternating with purple ornaments, adorned each table.

In a corner to the left of the head table, a separate table held the cake. It was everything she'd always dreamed of. Three tiers tall with stairways to another layer on each side and a small fountain underneath. She knew it was more cake than they needed, but she had decided she'd send the two side cakes back to the hotel to share with her coworkers. A DJ had set up in a back corner, and strains of a Mozart concerto played in the background.

"I am pleased to announce the arrival of the bride and groom, Mr. and Mrs. Ian Cavanaugh," the DJ called out as they entered.

The guests stood and clapped, offering handshakes as Lizzie and Ian passed by on their way to the front of the room. The rest of the wedding party had already taken their seats at the head table. The pastor, his wife, Emma, Ron, Colin, and Cassandra sat at a nearby table. Lizzie looked around for Stephen as Ian pulled out her chair for her. She found him in a corner by a door that she assumed went to the kitchen. Servers came out with chafing dishes and placed them on the buffet tables.

The DJ paused the music as Pastor Donovan stood and tapped on his glass to get everyone's attention. "The couple has asked that I say a blessing over the meal before we begin."

Lizzie twined her fingers with Ian's and bowed her head.

"Dear Lord, we thank you for bringing together Lizzie and Ian. We pray for your blessings upon their marriage. Help them to keep you at the center of their relationship, in good times and in hard times. Lord, bless this food. I understand there was quite a group effort in bringing it to us after some unforeseen circumstances. So, thank you for all those who came together to make this day possible. In Your holy name I pray, Amen."

The DJ turned on an instrumental version of "Over the Rainbow" while Stephen provided direction on the order for tables to visit the buffet. Lizzie and Ian led the way, followed by the rest of the wedding party.

"I'm starving, but I don't know if I can keep anything down," she whispered to Ian.

"Calm down, the hard part is over. Now we get to have fun. I know you don't want to miss the mashed potato bar."

Lizzie eyed the martini glasses filled with mashed potatoes and the bowls of toppings to choose from. She picked up a glass and began spooning on cheese and bacon bits. "You're right. Those do look good."

"Hurry up, I'm dying back here," Jeffrey called from the end of the line.

"Hold your horses, the bride can take as long as she wants," Ian called back.

Lizzie moved forward, dishing small portions of vegetables onto her plate. At the end of the buffet, she bypassed the carving station, carrying her plate back to her seat. Ian joined her a minute later with a plate piled high with every item offered.

"Are you going to eat all that?"

He grinned and gave her a wink. "I have to keep my strength up."

She nudged him with her shoulder and reached for a spoon, digging into the mashed potatoes. The guests were now flowing from their tables through the buffet, many stopping by to offer their congratulations on the way back to their seats.

Looking out at the familiar faces mixed among the new family she was now a part of, warmed Lizzie. She was glad she'd decided to have the wedding in Florida. It would have been difficult for her Concierge Club friends to have taken time off work for an out of state ceremony. Her eyes met James' and she waved. He blew her a kiss and his wife, Melanie, waved back. She felt Ian's knee bump against hers.

"There's Michelle," he said out of the side of his mouth.

Lizzie searched the faces of the guests until her gaze found Jeffrey. He was seated next to a woman in a royal blue dress, her brunette hair swept up in a chignon. She laughed at something Jeffrey said, the merry sound carrying across the room. Several conversations halted as guests turned to look for the source of the laughter. Michelle covered her mouth, but the laughter continued in her eyes. Jeffrey leaned forward and took her hands in his.

"He looks happy with her, doesn't he?" Lizzie said.

Ian nodded. "She's so different from Camylle. I think that's a good thing for Jeffrey."

Jeffrey stood, pulling Michelle to her feet. She smoothed her dress and touched her hair.

"Looks like they are coming our way," Ian said.

Lizzie took a sip of water then dabbed at her mouth with her napkin. "We should go and meet them. I feel like a judge sitting behind this table."

Ian chuckled and pushed his chair back, then helped Lizzie out of her seat. "You're the best looking judge I've ever seen."

"Been in front of many judges have you?" She caressed his face. He took her hand and kissed it, then led her toward Jeffrey. The two couples met on the edge of the dancefloor.

"It's nice to see you again, Ian. Congratulations."

"It's good to see you, too, Michelle. I'd like you to meet my wife."

Lizzie extended her hand. "I'm so happy you could come today. I hope the four of us can get together for dinner sometime soon."

"I've been warned not to accept a free meal from you." Michelle grinned.

Lizzie knew right away she was going to like this girl, but she glared at Jeffrey. "I told you at Thanksgiving that was my last project for a while."

Jeffrey shrugged. "How long will that last when you watch HGTV every weekend?"

Ian wrapped an arm around Lizzie's waist and pulled her close. "I'll try to keep her away from that temptation."

"Where are you going for the honeymoon?"

Jeffrey groaned as soon as the words were out of Michelle's mouth. "Don't bother, he's not telling anyone."

"Even I don't know," Lizzie said.

Michelle raised an eyebrow. "Didn't that make it hard to pack?"

"If she doesn't have something she needs, we'll just buy it, but I don't think that's going to be a problem."

His confidence made Lizzie wonder if he'd somehow managed to check her suitcases. "I guess the specialties of the area will determine if I need something new. If we're going to Milan then I know I will need a few new pairs of shoes."

"Maybe you're going to France. You'd definitely need some French perfume then," Michelle said.

"All right, before this gets out of hand, I think we should start mingling with our guests." Ian slipped his hand into Lizzie's. "I want you to meet my Aunt Wanda."

"It was nice meeting you," Lizzie called over her shoulder as Ian pulled her away.

CHAPTER FIFTY-SIX

The next hour, Lizzie and Ian floated from table to table, thanking the guests for coming. Ian's family members offered Lizzie a warm welcome to their family, which was reciprocated for Ian by her cousins and aunts who had come in from North Carolina. When they reached the front of the room where Ron and Emma were seated, Lizzie sank into an empty chair to catch her breath.

"We haven't even started dancing and already I'm exhausted."

Emma patted her hand. "Would you like me to get you something to drink?"

"A diet soda would be wonderful." Lizzie slipped off her shoes and rubbed her feet.

"You know once the shoes are off, your feet will only hurt more." Stephen dropped into the chair Emma had vacated and handed her a drawstring bag. "I thought you might be wanting these."

"You are the best." She accepted the bag and removed a pair of white canvas tennis shoes with Christmas plaid ribbon for laces. With a sigh of relief she slipped them on and placed her heels into the bag. "Thank you for adding the gel inserts. My feet feel better already."

"We couldn't have you stumbling through your first dance." Stephen extended his hand for the bag.

"I haven't seen Chef Gustave or Patricia. I wanted to thank them for all their help. If you hadn't told me about the caterers canceling, I never would have known this spread was put together on the fly."

"Believe it or not, I think Chef is quite enamored with the head chef here at the Inn, although there were some heated words when he first arrived. I thought I would have to put out another fire, but they came to some sort of understanding and have been talking over a bottle of wine since the food was served."

"I have to see that." Lizzie stood and looked around for the entrance to the kitchen.

Stephen grabbed her elbow. "You don't want to go into the kitchen and risk ruining your dress. Plus, I'm pretty sure Chef would kill me if he knew I told you about his flirtation."

Passing up the chance to see Chef Gustave flirting, not just with a woman but another chef, was almost more than Lizzie could bear. She ran a hand down her dress and glanced toward the kitchen door.

"I think it's time for the first dance," the DJ announced. "If we could get the happy couple out on the dancefloor."

"That would be us, my love." Ian appeared at her side and swept her away from Stephen. As they approached the middle of the dancefloor he looked down at her, his sapphire eyes full of adoration pushing all other thoughts from her mind.

When the opening bars of piano and strings flowed over them, Lizzie felt her face flush. Their first dance had been a point of debate between them. The song now playing wasn't what they had agreed on, but rather the one song that expressed the feelings she'd long hoped a man would feel for her, a song she kept so closely guarded she hadn't even included it in her list of ideas.

"How did you know?" she whispered.

Ian pulled her close, resting his forehead on hers. "Haven't I wiped away your tears and tried to keep you safe and warm?"

They swayed to the music, eyes locked on each other. She felt his thumb brush across her cheek and realized he had caught the tears leaking from her eyes. She'd experienced happiness with him many times before, but at this moment she didn't know if her heart could contain the joy she felt.

As the song faded and the guests applauded, Lizzie and Ian kissed, a long, tender kiss that made her stomach flip. She didn't want to leave the comfort of his embrace.

"It looks like they might need one more song," the DJ said with a chuckle and Michael Bolton's version of "A Kiss to Build a Dream On" started playing.

Laughter rippled through the crowd. Lizzie couldn't help giggling herself as Ian led her in a waltz, complete with turns and dips. Breathless at the end of the song, she leaned against Ian, and met Jeffrey's gaze. He dipped his head in a small nod of approval.

"Let's hear it for Ian and Lizzie," and the DJ led the crowd in applause. "Many of you know about the tragedy that took Lizzie's parents from her several years ago, but she told me that she didn't want to skip the father-daughter dance."

With a squeeze of Ian's hand, she moved toward the table where Ron and Emma were seated. She extended her hand to Ron and he stood. Instead of returning to the dancefloor, though, he reached into his pocket and removed a silver charm bracelet. She recognized the charm hanging from it, the picture frame with her parents' photo inside that she'd had attached to her bouquet. Ron clasped the bracelet on her wrist, then kissed her hand. She pulled him into a tight hug before leading him out onto the dancefloor.

Again she was surprised when the music started. Choosing a song for this dance had been even harder than the first dance with Ian. She didn't want to disrespect her father by using any of the traditional father-daughter type songs, but Ron had become a father figure in her life, just as Emma a surrogate mother.

Somehow Nat King Cole's "Smile" seemed like the perfect fit now that it was playing. Ron led her around the floor, ending with an elegant spin that landed her in Colin's arms. The party then seemed to pick up speed, and before she knew it, the DJ was announcing it was time to cut the cake.

Three tiers of cake sat atop six pillars. The white frosting was wrapped with Christmas ribbon, cascades of holly berries falling between the layers. Lining the stairways leading to two single layer cakes were sprigs of fir and tiny plaid bows. Chef Gustave met Lizzie and Ian at the table and handed them a knife.

Lizzie and Ian posed for the camera, pretending to slice into the cake. When the pictures were finished, Stephen hurried to her side and helped her put on a red and black flannel shirt. She wore it backward to protect the front of her dress, and Stephen clipped it together in the back with a clothespin. Emma's laughter filled the room, but Lizzie wasn't taking any chances. Ian had won out and red velvet had been chosen for the cake.

Lizzie kissed Chef on the cheek. "You've outdone yourself. It's beautiful."

"*Mon chéri*, you are the beautiful one, even in that ridiculous shirt."

Cake slices were placed on a plate between Ian and Lizzie. She didn't know if Ian would be gentle or playful when he extended his hand toward her. They'd discussed this moment, but with the surprises she'd already experienced, she wasn't sure what to expect. She made a split second decision and *smushed* the cake into his face at the same instant he did the same to her.

Stephen handed them napkins, shaking his head and suppressing a smile. "Good thing we went with the shirt."

"Where's the wine? I need something to wash down the little bit that did get in my mouth." Lizzie looked over her shoulder to see Arnaldo pouring the wine himself.

"Sheila snuck me in as her plus one," he said in a low voice as he handed her a glass.

Ian twined his arm with Lizzie's and then drank the wine, accompanied by cheers from the guests. The instant they were untwined, silverware was tapped against glasses, demanding the couple kiss. Lizzie was happy to oblige and rose up on tiptoe to meet Ian's lips.

"I've been told I'm not allowed to play the chicken dance tonight," the DJ called out, "but that doesn't mean we can't still have a party. Who's ready to dance?" Guests flowed onto the dance floor to *98 Degrees*, "True to Your Heart"

CHAPTER FIFTY-SEVEN

Her face was flushed, her hair pulled up in a messy bun, and she was out of breath, but Ian couldn't remember Lizzie looking more beautiful than she did at that moment. They'd had a chance to visit with all their guests, to dance, eat, even catch a few moments alone. Now the party was winding down and many of the local guests who had to work the next day were starting to leave.

"I'm so happy you could come," Lizzie said as she hugged James.

He winked at her. "I told you it wouldn't be too long before you'd be making compromises with somebody."

Lizzie remembered the night the previous summer when she'd bemoaned her being single to James. She hadn't then found the house she ended up renovating and he'd told her to enjoy being able to do the house hunting on her own, without having to make compromises on what she was looking for. She'd met Ian a week later.

Sheila hugged Ian. "Have fun on the honeymoon. I'll keep things in order at the office."

"Thanks, Sheila." Ian thought about telling her he'd email her their itinerary in case she needed to reach him. "I'll check in with you in a week."

"You'll do no such thing. You have more important things to attend to the next couple of weeks."

"Don't you worry. I plan to focus all my attention on making the most of the time off."

"Merry Christmas," Sheila said. "I'll see you in the new year."

It took another twenty minutes for them to make the rounds saying goodbye. They left the Inn amid a line of guests blowing bubbles and both waved from the windows of the car as they were driven away, until the Inn disappeared into the darkness.

"It seems surreal that we are going back to my house, but it's now our home."

"We aren't going to your house yet, but don't worry, you'll have plenty of time to get used to the idea before I get moved in."

"If we aren't going home then where are we headed, my delightful man of mystery?" Lizzie laid her head on his chest.

"You'll just have to wait and see." He ran his hand through her hair. She'd let it grow out for the wedding, and he loved the curtain of gold that fell around her face, but he also missed the sassy curls of her shorter style. "This was a perfect day. You did a good job planning it."

"Are you going to tell me what happened before the wedding? Who had a broken tie and a stuck zipper?"

Ian chortled. "It was my zipper and Jeffrey's tie. He said he didn't remember how to tie a bow tie so he went with a ready-made version that clipped together in the back, but the clip broke. I had my dad ask every woman in the church if they had a safety pin before we turned to you. I didn't want you to worry."

"I was worried when the time to start came and went without anyone letting me know what was going on."

Ian tilted her face up so he could see her eyes. "You weren't worried I was backing out, were you?"

She ran a finger along his lips. "No, I never questioned that."

The car came to a stop. "We're here, Mr. Cavanaugh," the driver said.

Lizzie sat up and looked out the window. The driver exited and opened the door. Ian stepped out and reached back to help Lizzie. A bellman greeted them, but Ian waved him off. He led her into the lobby of one of the most luxurious resorts in Orlando. People stopped to stare as they passed by toward the elevator.

"Don't we need—"

"I checked in before the wedding." He pushed the call button and the elevator opened right away. Inside, he pressed the button for the top floor followed by the door close button. "Come here."

Lizzie stepped into his embrace and melted into his kiss. He could feel her heart pounding and held her tighter. "I don't think I've told you today how beautiful you are."

"You look pretty good yourself," she murmured.

The elevator opened and he led her down the hall. Outside the hotel room door he stopped and took both her hands in his. "I love you more than I can ever put into words. I promise to spend the rest of my life making sure you know how important you are to me. I won't ever intentionally hurt you and I will do everything I can to protect you."

"Maybe we should have written our own vows."

He could tell she was only half joking. "I'm not finished."

He leaned back against the door and took a deep breath. "I know how hard it was for you to let down your guard and open yourself to me. I won't ever take that for granted. We are starting a new life together, as partners. Everything that came before is past and has no power over us. I want you to know you can trust me, that I will always treasure you and respect you."

She placed a finger over his lips. "I know. You've seen into my heart and you've brought me joy that I never knew existed."

He pulled an electronic key from his pocket and slipped his hand behind his back to unlock the door. He stumbled when the door fell inward, regaining his footing before stepping back and pulling her inside.

EPILOGUE

Church bells tolled their call to Christmas Eve mass. Lizzie and Ian strolled down the brick street of Ortisei, Italy, the snow-capped Dolomites rising in the distance. They'd explored the quaint shops and cafes only once since arriving, yet she felt as if they'd known the city for years.

Lizzie snuggled closer to Ian and sighed. "This has been a perfect week."

Two children raced past, their laughter filling the space in between the bells.

"What have you enjoyed most?"

"Hmm, shopping in Milan was nice. My new boots are gorgeous. Of course there's also the spa at the hotel." She giggled when she looked up and saw Ian roll his eyes. "I think my favorite thing, though, has been spending time alone with you."

They stopped under a street lamp outside the church. Ian turned her to face him. "That's what I've enjoyed most too. I know life will be crazy when we go home next week, but I promise always to make time for just the two of us."

Lizzie put a gloved finger on his lips. "I don't want to think about going home, not just yet."

The church bells grew silent and strains of "O Come All Ye Faithful" wafted through the open church doors. He took her hand in his and kissed it. "Let's go inside."

She climbed the steps beside him and they passed through a tall doorway. Candles flickered at the front of the church and in the hands of every worshiper. A young boy greeted them with unlit candles, pointing them toward a pew in the back that still had some empty seats. A weathered old lady gave them a gap-toothed smile and tipped her candle toward Lizzie's, the flame catching in seconds. By the time Ian's candle was lit, a new song had started, but Lizzie didn't recognize the melody.

Italian voices rose and fell all around them. She closed her eyes, hoping to impress the sound into her memory. Ian slipped his arm around her and she stepped closer. "Thank you," she whispered.

He kissed the top of her head then the music changed to another familiar tune, "Joy to the World". They lifted their voices in song and the old lady gave Lizzie an approving nod.

The candles Lizzie and Ian held had burned halfway down before the songs came to an end. When "Silent Night" began to play on the organ, people rose and streamed from their seats. Lizzie and Ian followed them out into the square where the only lights were the flickering flames of the congregation. Lizzie wondered if the street lamps normally went off after midnight or if this had been done for the service. She noticed she now stood next to a smartly dressed middle-aged man who sang in German.

There was silence after the song ended and candles were blown out. Even the children were quiet as they followed their parents home. Lizzie looked up and found the sky glistening with thousands of stars; a quarter moon hung over the church steeple.

"I am the luckiest woman in the entire world to have found you."

"I'm the lucky one." He leaned over and nuzzled her neck. "Even if I do have to spend the rest of my life doing home improvement projects."

ACKNOWLEDGEMENTS

I appreciate all of the support I've received from my readers and hope you enjoyed this final installment of the *Seasons of Faith* series. There are a number of people who helped make this series a reality and there are not enough words to express how thankful I am to each one of them, but I hope that they know how much I value their feedback and support.

Many thanks to my beta-readers, DiVoran and Pam, my editor, Clive, my proofreader, Faith, my cover designer, Laura, and my parents who've done everything from feeding me when I'm in the zone to picking apart scenes that just don't work. Special thanks to Nicole at Floral Creations by Dawn. I'm a very visual person and she took the time, not only to discuss floral arrangements, but also show me several options that helped with the design of the wedding floral.

I'm eternally grateful to God for instilling in me the love of books and giving me guidance as I write. Writing these books has helped me grow in my relationship with Him and I hope they will do the same for others.

If you'd like to see some of the photos that helped inspire Lizzie and Ian's wedding, please visit my Pinterest page at:
http://www.pinterest.com/itsrebekahlyn.

If you would like to learn more about my books please become a fan of my Facebook page at:
http://www.facebook.com/AuthorRebekahLyn

You can also follow me on Twitter @RebekahLyn1, or visit my website, RebekahLynBooks.com. If you love food and would like to find some of the recipes from my books check out my blog at:
http://www.rebekahlynskitchen.wordpress.com